CHILD
OF THE
UNIVERSE

* * *

JLF SULLIVAN

ISBN-13: 9798571071765
ISBN-10: 9798571071765

Cover design by: JLF Sullivan
Library of Congress Control Number 1-9911177051
Printed in the United States of America

For my sister Amanda,

a true child of the Universe

PREFACE

In 2017 my entire life came crashing down on me like a rogue wave. My family and I fled Hurricane Irma, only to return and find our home and businesses destroyed by the devastating Category 4 storm. For over a year we had no choice but to raise our children on our front lawn, surrounded by mountains of toxic debris, as we waited for the help our government and insurance companies promised us through lying teeth. With no other options, we began to sort through the toxic remains to see what of our life could be salvaged and rebuilt. It felt like we had been abandoned and left to rot in the festering remains of the life we had worked so hard for.

A few months into our ordeal, I woke up one morning to find the vision in my right eye was nearly gone. It looked like a large crescent shape was burned into my sight. My doctors informed me I had developed a condition called Pseudotumor Cerebri, and my loss of sight was due to pressure on my brain from an excess of cerebrospinal fluid. I was told the condition mimics a brain tumor and could lead to permanent blindness and stroke. Doctors are still not sure what causes this condition, but I believe my toxic exposure during the hurricane's aftermath was an instigating factor. For months I tried many medications and invasive procedures to reduce the swelling around my brain. After several failed attempts to control my vision loss using the best care my insurance was willing to pay for, I was offered to try a different approach.

In the fall of 2018, I first tried a Quantum Healing Hypnosis Technique session with Practitioner Sarah Breskman Cosme. We had known each other through our children and had a friendly relationship, so when Sarah offered the QHHT session I was trusting in her guidance. I had never heard of QHHT, but I had always been intrigued by the subject of past life regression. I had not understood up until that point, that hypnotic regression could be used to treat physical ailments in one's life. I was open minded and willing to try this unorthodox approach. I needed to find something that would help, as I feared how my worsening condition would affect my young children as well as the ability to rebuild my home and business.

In the aftermath of my first QHHT session, I

felt an immense relief of pressure from behind my eyes and felt a wave of stress lifted from my body. Within a few months, my eyesight returned and I began in many ways to see myself clearly for the first time. Now that the door to my mind had been opened, I wanted to know more. Over the next two years, Sarah guided me on numerous QHHT sessions, each bringing new light and understanding to a life I believe I lived on Earth before documented history. While I am usually a very private person, the past life we discovered is one that I am compelled to share, as I believe the process of uncovering it has as much healing power in it for others as it did for me.

Every day I am grateful for this experience I have had, and am now even thankful for the rogue wave that crashed into my life. Without it, I would have been stuck in a destiny not meant for me. I have found my true self through this process, as well as what may possibly be an alternative understanding of our origin on this planet. The story that follows is based on my past life regressions with Hypnotist Sarah Breskman Cosme, and the transcripts of our recorded sessions from 2018-2020.

JLF Sullivan

PROLOGUE

I always knew it would end with me. Instinct does not lie, and it does not do well to be ignored. My grandmother did her best to instruct me on how to ignore that feeling, to push it aside and separate myself from this empty version of my destiny. She believed it was possible, as she claimed to have felt this ominous curse in the early days of her reign as Queen of our land. "You must close your eyes and feel yourself float above it. This is not the only version of your destiny, you are the chooser of your world" she would say while guiding my mediation. I wanted nothing more than to please her, so I swallowed my truth. Instead, I now see that I should have embraced it and chosen to break eons of tradition so that the millions lost from my submission might have lived. I was the last conduit for my people. I failed them, and for that alone I am deeply sorry.

Perhaps it was best that this story has remained locked away within me since the great Cataclysms. But now my story can no longer stay buried alive within me, it must rest once and for all. It is my hope that by sharing this with you, my story will free us from this cycle of destruction we have become entangled in, for it is from the ashes of our past that the new and present civilization has arisen. We have been here before, and we have failed tragically. Maybe you too have dreamt of the great wave of Amun, it's towering greatness only to become your watery tomb. Or perhaps the mysteries surrounding the destruction of Atlantis have pulled your attention time and time again. It is my greatest wish that we may come to remember and understand our lost history so we may break free from the amnesia surrounding our humble beginnings.

There is something you cannot deny, something that you have felt for all your days that tells you that you are connected to something greater. The lives we live now and those of the long-forgotten past will begin to show their true relationship as we together journey back to the lands of Amun and Atlantis. I will do my best to explain why I did the unspeakable thing I did, and how I saw no other option for us to continue as we were. Between us there is great history. Our lives, souls, and blood intertwined from the moment of our earthly beginning. Soon, you might see that this world around us is a gift we have been given, a chance to do things right once and for all so that humankind might finally shift forward into the unknown. To ascend has always been our destiny, but as you digest my story you will come to understand that we do not always find our way the first time we try.

PART ONE

Beginnings

BEGINNINGS

The Land of Amun was home to over sixty million souls that lived within its island borders. Majestically floating in the aqua waters of the South Pacific, Amun stretched for nearly 3,000 miles from its furthest ends. Rolling hills traveled from coast to coast and produced an endless abundance of beauty and flavor in the fertile soil. The trees canopied their branches into woven blankets of flowers that provided shade for the well-traveled roads that crossed my homeland. The flowers were vibrant and welcoming, and as such reverberated in the lives of those who gazed upon them. With the rising of the sun, our highway of flowers would turn bright yellow and then darken as the day grew long, only to retire in the evening as a blood red blossom. Around the coastline lay beaches of pebbles made smooth from the ocean's fury. The smooth stones presented themselves in an array of natural colors and when warmed by the sun, felt therapeutic under the tired feet of those who pulled their livelihood from the water. The sea that surrounded Amun was very calm and presented a low tumble as it lapped away at the shore's colorful stones. Around us there was always a breeze, a sweet smelling current that travelled across the hills and brought a refreshing purity to each breath.

We were a peaceful people, a nation with no need for conquest and domination. People would commonly greet each other by saying "halofa" which meant "my love to you." This was said to loved ones as well as strangers, and brought a sense of value to each and every one of our inhabitants. During the rule of my family, the homes of Amun were secure and our people felt safe in our public centers. All nearby land masses were held under our protection and remained autonomous colonies that modeled our ideals and values. Amun held seven great cities and a multitude of growing colonies that lay beyond the border of the sun and the sea. Within the megalithic stone walls of our capital city, Lymuria, the masses congregated for trade, learning, and pleasure.

We had everything one could want to live out their existence happily, and so the masses did. The people of Amun progressed towards enlightenment in its many forms. An ancient energy source that had been gifted from early settlers from the stars created a continuous vibration of immunity from sickness to all our island inhabitants. Fairness was a priority in our society, as trivial differences did not carry much weight on our minds. Growing up there was the most beautiful experience that will forever be ingrained into my being.

Much of my early life was spent within the perfectly fitted stone walls of our royal palace. I was secluded from others early on and for good reason. My bloodline held very ancient powers that had been handed off from generation to generation, originating from the earliest travelers to colonize Earth. Just like my earliest ancestors, I was born with the ability to manipulate crystals and use their energy. The women of my line used this gift to communicate with our ancient ancestors, so we might guide our great nation with the wisdom of those who came before. The most powerful of all the crystals we used were the Red Crystals. Within our palace on a perfectly cut stone altar built ages before my time, our assemblage of Red Crystals were gathered and arranged in an altar to the Divine Universe. After meditating with my hands on the Red Crystals, I could channel an ancient energy that would inform of things that have transpired and things that have yet to materialize. When I performed this meditation, I was often guided by the spirit of a young girl, her name was Oona. As a lonely child I would beg her to come to my world and play with me. Oona assured me that one day we would be together, but for now I have many things I am meant to do with my time on Earth.

Where I lived, it was a very private and secluded area where only certain people could go.

The immense stone palace was built thousands of years ago by our ancestors from the stars. When one would go inside its entrance, it felt like the building was swallowing you whole. The grey stone floors were cold and polished brightly from thousands of generations of use. Slight indents from wear in the stone steps cupped your feet as you climbed the grand staircase into the welcoming hall, and headed into the private quarters that housed my family. Down a long corridor there was an arched stone doorway leading into my sleeping quarters. The lengthy passageway was thick with perfectly fitted dark grey stone that intricately encircled the sconces above that illuminated my walkway. In my bedroom there were many luxuries, my most prized was a circular mat on an elevated platform that backed against a melted stone wall. There was no equal for the soft material that was used in its creation. I remember clearly how soft the covering for the overstuffed mat was and how lush it was to sink into its billowy depths after my royal training.

In this room I found solitude and was able to be myself. There was always a gentle breeze that blew in keeping me cool and free of the burden of insects and their stings. Some of my earliest memories as a young girl bring me back to this room where I would lie in bed at night and trace my finger along the strange grooves of the melted rocks walls. My grandmother would tell me stories of how these lines came to be as I would lay in my bed at night fighting sleep. She believed our ancient ancestors used a lost technology to melt stone and create our great cities and numerous monoliths.

With my finger I would trace the thin lines that connected the molded rock and listen to her benevolent voice fill my ears and mind. My grandmother said the rock wall was made using a Red Crystal and a device that could be held in the hand and pointed at a rock surface. "It could burn off a piece of the rock very quickly and fit it together very precisely while levitating it in the air," she explained as her hands folded together into a triangular shape to mimic the device. While this technology was lost to time, the Red Crystals we used in our private lessons were the same Red Crystals once used to create the walls that surrounded me.

An intricate system of mirrors had been built into the massive structure, allowing for sunlight in the day and firelight in the evening to naturally illuminate the many dark passageways of the palace. Glowing glass orbs sat upon sconces that lined the dark stone corridors. These luminating mechanisms built long before my time were not the only marvels of the palace. The construction would retain its coolness on the hotter months inside so that the further into the building you would wander, the cooler it would be. This was assisted by a gravity fed water system plumbed into the rock from a fresh spring that was once used by our earliest ancestor, the Divine Mother Evi. The water was believed to have healing properties and so we began each day by giving her thanks and breaking our nightly fast with large stone cups of this mineral elixir.

My earliest memories are dominated by the time I spent staring into the large stained glass window of a thousand flowers in our grand receiving room. The early morning sun would bounce around the walls reflected off the flower of life design that geometrically bloomed across the domed glass ceiling. As I stared at the flowers' intricacies, the pattern would put me into a trance as I would repeat the words my grandmother communicated to me: "Love is eternal. Where earthly love exists we see a reflection of the great divine love. Connect to that love, feel it wrap around your head and encapsulate you." As she repeated herself my head would begin to feel as though it was larger and floating up, up into the sky, but somehow covered in stone all at once. The Red Crystals I held in my hands would get very hot and would sometimes leave blisters in the center of my palms. "That just means you are doing it correctly," my regal grandmother would say with pride as she examined the insides of my hands.

As I grew older, my sessions with my grandmother began to change and allowed for an unparalleled education. I was introduced to a different world through our meditations. At first, my grandmother began to direct my floating spirit with her suggestive voice and showed me the many ways I could travel in this new world. There was a vast emptiness there that felt exhilarating to behold. I found happiness in this place and enjoyed its exploration, until one day I came across a large wooden door I had not noticed during our previous meditations. It stood alone, out of place amongst the greenery and raw nature. It looked very old and made me feel uneasy. "Pull the door open," my Grandmother gently advised. As I pulled its heavy metal ring towards my chest I felt instant regret when I gazed at the fury that lay inside. Water came roaring at me, sweeping me into bodies and debris that piled up against my face and chest, I could not scream, I could not breath. It took my grandmother a few moments to realize something was wrong, and by the time she acted and pulled me from the trance, the damage had been done. I was shocked so deeply that I did not speak a sound for the better part of a year.

My mother, Queen Sunisa, was very cross with my grandmother over my impediment. "How could you let this happen? Do you know what I have been through to get us here?" she roared at her mother as I watched from behind a curtain. I remember her voice was so powerful I was too scared to move, even breathe. After my mother had cast off some of her anger, my grandmother calmly reminded her that it can not be controlled what our ancestors wanted me to see, and that if it was revealed, then it must be for a reason. My mother refused this explanation and without saying goodbye, left on a trip to oversee a new colony the very next day. When she returned, I had made great improvements in communicating, but still felt very ashamed of my lagging stutter. I still remember her face as I attempted to greet her for the first time in months and got stuck on the word for mother. It ripped me apart inside to see her firm smile fall downward, and her eyes avoid my line of sight. I was so upset I began to spend more and more of my time alone in the other world. I was careful to never open the door again, but it always remained there in my journeys, a leaking reminder of the damage my curiosity would lead to.

Even as a young child I remember the deep reservations I had over my future as Queen of the Land of Amun. There was no doubt that I would one day become Queen and inherit the right to rule. These powers had been bestowed upon my bloodline for thousands of generations, from mother to daughter we passed on what was called "The Gift of the Stars." My dark coiled hair held a sacred streak of silver that grew from the right side of my temple. It was the same in my mother's hair, and grandmother's, and stood as a constant exhibit of the deep connection our bloodline held to our earliest ancestors and their emblematic silver hair. It was tradition dating back from our time of origin that a Queen of Amun would begin her reign in her twenty-fifth year. It was expected that her span of rule would last the next twenty five years. After the next took power, you served as head of the Advisory Council that helped govern our far reaching land and its overseas borders.

From the day you were born, until the day you died and had your face carved into our commemorative cliffside relief, your life was mapped out for you down to the last detail. There was little room to alter from this, and any deviance from the grand plan was seen as a warning of predicament to come for our people. The people of Amun were creatures of habit and found their security in these rituals. For most of our nation's history, the tradition of reign had been successfully passed down from mother to daughter, over and over again ensuring the prosperity of Amun, that is, until me.

During the rainy season of my seventh year, a careless chambermaid chatted with my caregiver as they cleaned my quarters, not realizing I was practicing my crystal pendulum quietly in the windowsill within earshot. They spoke of my sister, an older child of my mother's I had never known of. I asked the crystal I held if this was true, and instead of swinging in one direction for yes, or another for no, it suddenly stopped swinging and hung eerily still on its chain. With my mother once again gone to oversee the development of a new colony, I ran to my grandmother looking for an explanation. Her face pained and darkened in color as she sat me on her lap. With great trepidation, she explained that my mother had birthed a daughter three years prior to my birth, her first-born, her everything. The child was called Aruna, her name meant the first ray of light to come from the dawn. My grandmother assured me that Aruna had been greatly loved and cherished by all who surrounded her. On a steaming hot day, during her second year, the small Princess was taken to the ancient Step Well to cool off in the pool of water collected in its basin. The steep white limestone steps went down deep into the earth and led to a bubbling spring that collected into a pool often played in by local children.

I learned my sister had been a very independent child and enjoyed counting the steps as she descended them with my grandmother. Everyone watched it happen, and there was nothing any of them could do as the small Princess slipped and fell in slow motion. She did not fall far, but landed strangely and twisted her neck. It happened, and it could not be undone. There were records of the mourning in our land lasting for over six months. During that time, no one could marry, no one could celebrate. The stiff measures did not need to be enforced, the nation mourned alongside its Queen. Many of our great populus were made nervous and spooked by this sudden break in tradition. For the first time in a long time, my grandmother explained, they were scared of the future.

My mother knew what needed to be done,

and an impregnation ceremony was held as quickly as it could be arranged. There was no one more prepared for the role she was taking on than my mother, and the death of her child was the only thing she could not control in her reign. Everything that had been expected of her she fulfilled to the utmost pinnacle of perfection. When she lost her first child, it was more than losing a child, she lost our legacy. In her eyes, it showed weakness and a break that could never be mended. She was no longer the great leader they prophesied her to be, her destiny revoked, and now worse, she was one to be pitied. This hardened her in such ways that she naturally began to turn away from people and human attachments.

As her stomach grew with my life, her people rallied around her once more, grateful for this second chance. When my birth time arrived, my grandmother assured me that I was celebrated in all the land and cherished just as much as my sister. Even though I yearned for my mother in my infancy, she could not nourish me. Her heart had broken into a thousand pieces, and she no longer trusted herself to be someone's mother. She called me Kala, a name meaning princess, and handed me off to my grandmother.

My mother was a broken woman who somehow managed to make it look like nothing had ever happened to her, like a broken flower vessel beautifully mended with gold. Our relationship was very difficult from the first day of my arrival.

She did not make it easy to love her, yet I did. She was cold, distant, critical and lacked a familial bond that I craved. She was not cruel or mean spirited, she just was not there. My mother's sense of duty and sacrifice for her people ran deep, and her role as ruler allowed her to intentionally keep herself busy to avoid me. As the years passed, I found it peculiar that no one commemorated or even mentioned my sister's name. It was as if with my birth she was erased from their vocabulary, and they spoke only of my future reign to come. I realized later that this was because they were afraid to make me feel inferior to my destiny, but I always found it odd they never brought up the act that led to the only reason I was born.

As a past Queen of Amun, my grandmother was also very busy but found time for me because she felt that if quality time was not spent with me then I would not be prepared for my governing role ahead. My grandmother's subjects addressed her as Queen Rajini, a name properly bestowed upon her at birth, meaning "the guiding light of the moon" in our language. In the time of her reign, she was celebrated for being a very wise and fair ruler. During our time together she would share her anecdotes and experiences from her period of rule to explain how I could be the best version of myself when I would one day govern. During her early years as ruler, my grandmother dealt with a famine in the Land of Amun when rain did not fall during the expected springtime inundation. The crops withered and died and replanting led to a weak harvest.

Through a series of convalescent meditations she saw a new way to irrigate crops that allowed for their roots to grow within a large container of stone that was fed by the water made dirty by fish. Only certain crops were advised to be planted in this method, and when implemented it produced remarkable results. Food grew fast and plentiful, and was tastier than ever before. Queen Rajini's ability to lead the people of Amun through this uncertainty gave her much respect from her people and as a result, statues carved in her image were prolific throughout our empire.

On a hot summer day during my ninth year, I walked midday with my grandmother to the same Step Well where my sister Aruna had died. We arrived at the blindingly white limestone platform and began our descent down the many staircases of perfectly cut stone, zig zagging our way to the glistening pool of water that lay at the bottom. As we descended the many steps, the air around us grew cooler and moist as we left behind the oppressive heat above. At the bottom I could see there were many others there, mostly mothers who lounged nearby as their children splashed and sang songs of friendship. Excitement surged within my veins at the thought of making a real friend. I began to skip steps and hurry downward towards the gathering of children, when I suddenly lost my balance and slipped off the side of the stone steps.

I caught my grandmother's eye and saw her look of terror as I began to fall so very near where my sister's accident had happened years ago. My arms shot out wildly, reaching around me for anything I could hold on to, but there was nothing but air to fill my desperate grasps. I felt a cold jolt of electricity shoot through my body as I closed my eyes and braced for a painful impact, with the stone floor many feet below me.

Confusion set in as I opened my eyes and felt only a fraction of the pain I believed a fall of such measure would create. As I shakily took in my surroundings, I could see that instead of the hard stone floor, a bony boy my age had broken my fall. It was no act of heroism, I had surprised him, as well as his mother who had accompanied him there. I could hear his mother yell out for her son's safety as I slipped and fell on him. Quickly, she pulled me off him and was about to chastise me, when his mother looked up and saw my grandmother towering above us. The boy's mother immediately fell silent, but was quickly embraced by my grandmother in a gesture of thanks. The boy's dark hair covered a wound on his forehead that was trickling blood down the side of his face. We locked eyes as I struggled to breathe, as the air had been knocked from my lungs. Even though my grandmother raged and chastised me publicly for my error, it was as if time stood still for me and my new friend. He pushed his pin straight hair behind his ear revealing the place where the sharp edge of the stone step had stolen some of his skin. That scar would clearly remain on his face until the last time I ever saw him, it always stood out as a reminder of my debt to him.

The boy who broke my fall was the son of one of my sworn guards and had hoped to catch a glimpse of his father on our journey to the Step Well. Even though he was the same age as me, he was very tiny but also very strong. As he helped me up, he took my hand and we walked to the bottom of the Step Well and played in the cooling water. We splashed and laughed, and for the first time in my life, I felt I had made a real friend. He asked my name, and without blinking I answered "my name is Kala, I am the future Divine Ruler to the Kingdom of Amun." He laughed in my face as a response to my properness. "My name is Leo, I am the future friend of Kala, Ruler of Amun." I was not sure how to take his sense of humor. Not many people joked with me, and it was an unfamiliar feeling to want to laugh at something so proper and ingrained. But I did smile and even began to laugh, and it only made him laugh harder. I felt at ease with Leo so I showed him a trick that I could do with my mind. It was an illusion, where I could take a stick and make the stick turn into a snake for a few moments, just long enough to scare someone. My magic did not truly turn the stick into a snake, but changed another's perspective of the object for a few moments.

Leo made it clear from the first time I performed this trick that he did not like snakes, and so this began a tradition of me inundating him with stick snakes when we played. I remember the first time Leo saw the stick snake slithering towards him. He jumped into a decorative water garden built into the Step Well and plucked a pink lotus from its watery bed and threw it at the snake. The bloom hit the snake and banished it back into the stick form it preferred. From that day on he always brought me pink lotus, in case the snake should return. As we grew older and left our childish bodies behind, he would still bring me pink lotus flowers and I would still chase him off with snakes, especially when he appeared too affectionate and too wanting.

As children, Leo came over quite often to play because they trusted my life to his father and they trusted his mother as a woman of good standing in our society. My mother was not around often and my grandmother quite busy, so a trusted companion to fill my time was seen as a blessing. In the mornings our time was spent learning in our separate ways: mine within the walls of the palace, and Leo's within the walls of one of our nearby public institutions. All of the children of Amun were expected to attend our schools until the age of sixteen, and learned a variety of skills and concepts to promote independent thinking and innovation in our society. In the early evening, when our studies would be done, we would meet up in the grand receiving room of the palace. With my guards in tow, we would visit many different nearby water sources and practice our swimming and diving maneuvers. Leo would try to impress me and his father by catching little silver and red fish with his bare hands. His father would laugh at their puny size and throw his head back and eat them whole as he joked about what a poor snack they made.

Sometimes Leo would bring his favorite game with him, it was held in a wooden box that had little cups carved into the lid. I remember the purpose was to get rid of all of the polished stones given to each player, but I have lost the rest of the rules to time. Leo tried for ages to teach me, but the many rules seemed to be hopelessly complicated. He was persistent that I should learn this game, a gift that had come from a far off land one of his family members had journeyed to.

I was about to lose all interest in this game when one day I beat him, and we became very competitive in all we did after that. Everything we did, we had to outdo each other. There was no end to it. We would even climb the massive hexagonal volcanic columns that lined the many gardens of the palace and see who could climb highest. My guards would form a human mat beneath me as I dared to go higher than Leo until his father would call out his name and with nothing more than a look, cause his son to begin an immediate descent to the garden floor.

We were truly blessed children to have the run of the royal gardens of Amun as our playground. The reign of my mother, Queen Sunisa, produced magnificent gardens, true masterpieces to delight the senses. Each plant was chosen with extreme detail and cared for by an array of gardeners who were recognized heavily for their beautiful contribution to our community. All of the gardens at the palace were supported by the same gravity fed water system our ancient ancestors had laid into the palace's foundation. Each garden was not complete without its own unique water feature. Some of the gardens even housed gnarled trees so big that nature had created a wooden cave within them.

I had been informed that many of the strange looking trees in the gardens had been brought as seeds from the old world, the home planet of our ancestors from the stars. These were considered special trees and were only grown in the palaces most secretive of gardens. They were not the original trees first planted by the ancient colonists, but were their descendants, as tens of thousands of years had passed since their initial sprouting. Some of the mysterious tree seeds were hooked shaped and unlike others I had seen in our wide reaching land. The rare seeds were stealthily kept and continuously replanted, so the true taste of the home planet was never forgotten.

My favorite fruit was a sweet, heavy flavor

full of jasmine and rose. Deep and full of life, when its fruit ripened it was considered a great delicacy and a rare treat to be given one. The seeds were all removed before serving for fear they may lose out on the opportunity to plant one more of these great trees in our nation. At night, the gardens would smell entirely different than during the daytime. The heavy musk that would drift into my bedroom at night always pulled me outside onto my starlit terrace to imagine which garden the mysterious perfume was drifting from.

It was on a beautiful morning during the dry season of my fourteenth year when I began my warrior training. I remember being very excited to start, though I had never really been that inclined towards learning the Moves of War, as our people called it. We trained in a dance-like formation at first to make us swift and light on our feet. It also molded our muscles into shape and positively charged their muscle memory with the fluid movements. I worked with a long metal pole learning different kinds of swift movements. The shaft was all wooden at first, and then topped with metal after a few months.

Some attached knives and others attached balls with spikes to the end of their pole. The best moved onto entirely metal poles that carried sharpened blades on either end. Metal workers were very proud of their crafted blades in our culture. They were reserved only for the best at this art form. I was surprisingly good at maneuvering the pole against others. I had wide shoulders that were strong and used this to my advantage. I was told I took after my mother in this manner, and this pushed me to be perfect in my form with hopes it would please her.

My training taught me leverage and timing in battle, with a focus on structure not strength. We learned the Moves of War not because we were a warring people, but to promote longevity amongst our society through activity and exploration. While we did have an army, most of our soldiers never saw battle. Many went out exploring by boat in the name of Amun. It was not to find people to hurt and pillage, it was to examine our surroundings so we could keep the motherland safe. At times, we would hear word of a massacre in some far off colony of Amun. Usually some squabble over resources that had grown thin and provoked madness. To show we had zero tolerance for this kind of behavior, we would have to send out our warriors and bring the culprits to justice for what atrocities had been committed. This was a rare occurrence, but even still, we trained and kept our bodies prepared for anything.

I practiced the Moves of War each morning on my private beach by the water. There was a very narrow sandy strip alongside calming ocean water outside my bedroom, and for a few hours I would work until the sun's heat was too much. This beach was my place to be alone with my thoughts. This was the place I went to escape what was expected of me. Near the gentle shoreline was a set of precisely cut stone steps below an arched stone doorway that led to my private terrace and into my bedroom. This was my mother's room before me, and my grandmother's room before her. One day it will be my daughter's room. But for that moment, it was my room, and a prison it was to me in many ways I did not realize at the time. On the beach, I swung my pole and I was free for a moment at a time.

On a stormy day during my fifteenth year, I was called into the glass domed garden of my Grandmother's adjoining quarters. There was a beautiful cascading waterfall that plummeted down from a stone precipice above, and fell down like a sheet of water in the middle of the garden. Surrounding us were masses of tropical flowers with reds, purples, oranges, and yellows all dotted throughout the luscious greens of varying vibrancy. There were colorful fish floating happily in the pond that served as a reservoir for the waterfalls flow. The flow churned the water up and spread the sweet smell of fresh water and jasmine in the air. My grandmother proudly housed very elegant looking birds that were white with red and yellow tips on the end. The regal birds floated around us and looked as though they had elaborate feathered hats on.

In this relaxing environment, my grandmother was able to put me into a deep trance. I stared at a candle while she chanted the ancient words repeatedly, and then all of a sudden information materialized in blocks in my inner mind. My spirit friend Oona appeared and was glowing with happiness. As she guided me through this information, I was at first confused but then I saw clearly that this was not my first time on this planet, nor my last. Oona showed me that my soul has been linked with many I know around me, my family, friends and even those yet to be born. Our souls have agreed on what we will do in this existence before our arrival on Earth, and the challenges we shall face have been chosen and agreed upon by all who interact.

A vision of my dear friend Leo drifted into my mind and caused a stir within me. I saw that I have a soul contract with my companion, and it is beautiful and full of thorns all at once. We are the worst kind of soul mates, destined to be torn apart. I felt the devastating isolation both our futures held in those few moments and decided to end my session with my grandmother for the day. Later that evening, Leo came to see me as after his studies as we had planned when we parted the day before. I told my guards I could not see him, I felt overwhelmingly responsible for our disheartening destiny. This was the first time I ever turned him away. I watched Leo's father tell him from afar that I would not see him. I will never forget the look on his face, disbelief and fury all at once. If only he knew how I did it to spare him the misery of what I saw for us.

It had been two days prior that we had shared a kiss for the first time. It had happened so naturally as we swam underwater on my private beach. We dove under the mellow waves and I lost sight of him. Panicked, I turned in circles looking for him and twisted one last time to find him face to face, trying to scare me with an odd expression. He had done this for years while we were children, but this time I felt an overwhelming compulsion to pull his face close to mine and kiss it. The water made it feel like our lips never even touched. Bubbles rose around us as Leo smiled in response to my forward gesture. He pointed his finger upwards towards the surface and we both swam up for air. On shore stood my guards carefully watching us, Leo's father held the deepest stare of all. We both realized then and there that under the waves was the most private place we would ever have, it was all we could ever have.

In the days that followed I plunged into a deep depression. I could not relax or think clearly and struggled to connect to the other worlds during our lessons. I felt the oppression of tradition weighing down on me. Sensing heaviness on my mind, my grandmother adjourned from our usual place of learning and led me to the stone labyrinth overlooking the sea behind our palace. "A place for the spirit to be reborn" is what she always called it as we would approach the Labyrinth's entrance. On the edge of a cliff overlooking the wide reaching ocean, there was a beautiful doorway made of stone that had been impeccably molded by the earliest architects of Amun.

Through this magnificent doorway we descended down the smooth steps chiseled from the white mountainside. A narrow walkway led to the circular stone platform that housed the labyrinth, which appeared to float above the ocean. Encircling its perimeter were large conch shells that had been cut very precisely by my ancestors to allow the emission of a special sound when the wind would hit their openings. The conch shells melody created a pleasant buzz in the air, a soothing vibration to guide one as they walked the Labyrinth in search of answers. Hearing the tones while walking the winding pathways would change your inner vibration, and open up inside of you the path to the answer that was trying to get to you.

As I walked the Labyrinth, I mulled over my recent developments with Leo and the possibilities of what the future might hold for us. No Queen of Amun had ever taken a mate; it was our tradition to rule alone. Our children were all born from a collective sample of the bravest and most compassionate of the men in our society, and little physical contact was truly ever had between the Queen and all others, even during our impregnations. This was what I was taught, and was told would be expected of me. I felt differently, but saw how that was not something I could negotiate. It was bad enough my existence was already a bad omen for my mother's reign, I could not risk the people not accepting another break from tradition. No matter how much I insisted this was my obedient future, the Labyrinth only provided me with a clearer picture of Leo. With this clear vision and new understanding, I asked Leo's father to send for him the next day after my training.

It did not take long for us to get into trouble. We had no privacy and risked every secret kiss or touch we could. Leo's father eyed him suspiciously whenever he was being sneaky, threatening him without a sound. One evening he stayed late to watch the stars with me on my private terrace and was seen sneaking away by my mother. The Queen did not feel that it was appropriate for us to be together after that. She felt that we were getting too close and my decisions were being influenced by Leo. In her mind that was a red flag, a weed to be plucked from her perfect gardens. My mother firmly told me with a face quietly exploding that my decisions should be influenced by the women who ruled before me, not the son of a guard. That was what my mother's belief was, and there would be no break in tradition if she was the one who was destined to fulfill the long awaited prophecy.

Unfortunately, my grandmother agreed with my mother and Leo was immediately sent far away to train with the Naacal Brotherhood. There he would be trained mentally, physically, and spiritually by a guild that was a keeper of our documented history and legends. The Naacal's collaboration was an ongoing effort to continuously keep the history of the land of Amun. Leo's posting would serve as a credit to his family, as it was a very respected and revered position in our society. My mother asserted that there was no need to make ill will with the families of my guards. I was sure Leo had gone unwillingly, there was nothing less he wanted in life than to join a group that practiced isolation. Leo was loud and confident, his laughter could be heard from far away and was easily identifiable. I feared the strict Naacal Temple would break his spirit, and I would forever lose the sound of that echoing laughter.

The Naacal repository they took him to was located in the second most populous city of Amun, far from my home in the capital of Lymuria. In the center of this town, high above the homes and businesses, was a large circular stone structure that housed millions of the Naacal's records that detailed our people's existence. I had travelled there once before as a child, I remember in front of the Naacal's structure there was a large brass bell shaped like a rounded step pyramid, identical to the one I often passed in Lymuria. The bells were part of a warning system created during the early days of Amun, and allowed for a deep vibrational tone to be heard for miles around, and signaling to nearby towns of impending danger.

Inside their circular stone structure there was an endless library filled with numerous clay tablets, as well as scrolls and historical artifacts from our ancient ancestors. Those who joined the Naacals were mostly men, but there were certain women who joined if they felt a calling. One was expected to live a life of quiet solitude in this facility and those who joined would spend their days fasting, meditating, and writing. They could not marry and they could not have families, as they were expected to dedicate their lives to the history they were sworn to protect. I knew what being sent to this place meant for Leo and I was devastated. He was delivered to their care before I was given a chance to say goodbye, and from there we are both separated and forced to move on with our lives.

My mother began to spend more time with me after Leo was sent away. Perhaps she felt guilt when she saw the hurt in my eyes. Even though her perfect face revealed nothing, her actions felt as though she wanted to make up for some invisible mistake she refused to acknowledge. It felt as if she was reclaiming me with the quality time she was initiating. We began to do new types of meditations that I was of age to learn, trances that required the use of mind-altering substances to communicate with other realms most effectively. I welcomed these new lessons and the break from the bleak reality they provided. I first learned how to concoct the mind-altering liquid that was derived from muddling the juices of a water root and a cactus fruit.

The body had to be cleansed and anointed with a special oil before the liquid was consumed. When taken with a group, the liquid would be passed in an abalone shell from highest ranking down to lowest in the group, until all has been used and not a drop remained. I learned it was important to make just the right amount or the effect would be too powerful, and little would be comprehended of our ancestors' messages.

When administered properly and in the right company, the sanctified liquid allowed one to veer into another dimension that had an incredible euphoric quality to it. Many have gazed upon it and confused it for what some might call Heaven. It was an abundant dimension with an all-seeing eye presiding over it. When we mentally travelled there, we believed it was our dead ancestors who guided us. "Talking to the dead" was what my grandmother called it. We would travel there often and ask them questions to seek guidance in our empire's expansion. Countless visitors would travel from far away colonies to sit with us and ask questions as we sat in meditative trance. There was always an answer, though not all liked hearing the answers we provided. Sometimes, these sessions would become too tiring and repetitive. People wanted to know the same things over and over. Such creatures of habit can become frustrating to even the most experienced oracle.

To detox from these sessions there was a special aquatic ritual that needed to be performed. I would stand below an ancient stone fountain cut on such perfect angles that it created a veil of warm water trickling down my spine. The water there flowed from the sacred spring of Mother Evi that had materialized during the ancient time of our great upheaval. While holding a Red Crystal and meditating as the water relaxed your spine, you could connect with a different place, an empty darkness, and ask that your burden be lifted. Once you are free of the stress of others you may stay in this place as long as you need. There was an invisible library there that held the records of my familial line going back to Oona, the First Queen of Amun, and beyond. The energy of the omniscient library guided me to a specific memory, one they believed I was ready to receive.

In the earliest days of Amun there were two sisters of hybrid blood, one obedient and the other strong willed. To the outside world they seemed complete opposites, yet in their private lives they were inseparable, thriving off each other's differences. The sisters lived a blissful existence full of learning and wonder in their ancient seedling community founded by our ancestors from the stars. The elder sister Oona excelled in the spiritual traditions of her predecessors, while the younger sister Isa innovated these ideas and improved their surroundings with her scientific curiosity. Oona was doted on by her community, a mix of humans, colonists, and their hybrid offspring, while Isa often lived in her shadow and found no place amongst her people.

On the day of the Spring Equinox the sisters attended a great celebration held at the stone circle on their island. This was the one day a year visitors might journey through the natural vortex that would appear within the circle, a transportive energy they called the Chasm. While the community gathered to welcome the opening of the Chasm, there was a terrible shaking of the Earth that came without warning. The large stone monoliths trembled around them as crowds ran for safety from the sliding rock.

The stones had been carved to resemble people, and the trembling of the earth made it appear as if they danced in unison around the terrified sisters. Large blocks of obsidian that lined the top of the stone circle screeched a deafening tone as they began to slide back and forth above the surrounding stone figures. The sisters clung together in fear as the face of the stone giant began to topple into them. Their mother Evi lunged for her daughters and sacrificed herself by taking their place under the rock. Evi's final actions were to push her daughters to safety. Oona was pushed outward towards her people, and Isa was pushed inwards towards the activated Chasm's vortex.

When the Earth stood still again Oona realized she had escaped death, though her luck did not extend to all the inhabitants of the community. Many were killed during the upheaval, including all of the early settlers from the sky. Their homes and buildings were in heaps of rubble around them. From a crack that emerged in the rock responsible for crushing their mother Evi, sprang a curative water source that nourished the broken back to health. Much of the colonists' advanced technology from afar was lost, but the special Red Crystals brought from the home planet were spared. In order to preserve what was left of the seedling community, Oona cast aside her grief and led those spared in the upheaval. Through her self-sacrifice and guidance from the Red Crystals, she was able to create the growing, thriving empire that Amun was to become.

On the fateful day of the Spring Equinox, Isa travelled through the Chasm and found herself transported to a faraway room carved within the confines of a mountain. Around her stood a small grouping of tall men with long silvery beards and blue cloaks. They looked as old as the Earth and stood quite still amongst the stone pillars of the Chasm when Isa appeared. In all their earthly trials to begin a seedling community they had never seen the birth of a successful hybrid child. The sudden presence of a child of mixed blood was their ethereal sign that despite their previous failures, the great experiment would continue.

The Silver Beards possessed an ancient form of knowledge that created peacefulness within the human form. Their early experiences on Earth had shown them the need for such peace, and so they had *constructed a domed room within the mountain that they continuously charged with this peaceful energy. Isa was hysterical from her ordeal and journey, but when ushered inside the chiseled out room of peace, she felt quiet and contemplative. Once fully inside the rounded room, she could see the reason for her traumatic experience. The peaceful energy enveloped Isa and showed her the path her fate had now taken. She was now where she was needed most in the Universe.*

The humans that lived near the mountain were superstitious of the mountain and stayed away from the Silver Beards. The loss of the hybrid children had taken a large toll on the humans, and they no longer wished to subject themselves to the experiments of the star people. When Isa descended the mountain with the Silver Beards, the humans could not help but flock to Isa, the hybrid child. They were amazed by her knowledge and powers and felt a compulsion to dote on her. Isa was able to show them how beautiful it will be, how wonderous it can all be when we merge our worlds together. It was not long before she convinced the humans to rejoin the experiment so that other hybrids like her may live and use their abilities to better society.

Isa understood the Chasm was too unpredictable to attempt to return to her sister, and so she stayed with her new people. Under her leadership and innovation, they all found what they had been seeking. A large underground city was constructed in the mountain by the Silver Beards to protect Isa and their beloved experiment. Their tunnels dug into the Earth for miles and led into spacious openings that held finely carved homes for the humans and their hybrid children. When they felt their mission was complete, the Silver Beard's earthly forms disintegrated and they absorbed their eternal energy into the mountain, so that others might benefit from their peace.

My friend Oona appeared before me in her spirit form as I digested the block of information received from the Red Crystal. She told me that there would be times in my life when I would feel very alone, for this was the sacrifice I was expected to make for the betterment of our society. Oona reminded me that this was part of my soul contract, and had been chosen by me before I took this earthly body. I could not understand why I would have wanted to take on such a despairing roll in this lifetime. I became irate, and began to yell at my dear friend every objection I had held back until now. Her patient knowingness only infuriated me and I looked to leave the Library of Collected Knowledge. Oona imparted a final thought in my mind as I drifted back to my body. "It is important that you remember when you are separated from those you love, that your journeys will reunite at the end of this lifetime, as you too are a child of the Universe."

It was during the onset of my twentieth year that my ceremony of impregnation was arranged. Word was sent throughout Amun to nominate those who would be worthy of fathering my child and their future leader. I would not know who these men were until the night of the ceremony, a night I was anxiously dreading. I had no choice in who would be chosen, and I knew I must accept whomever was deemed worthy by my people. On the night of the next full moon, I was bathed, dressed and anointed in jasmine oil, then led into a special room in the palace that we did not use often. It was a circular room with a rectangular slab of stone in the center that rose up to my belly. The ample slab was smooth, flat and cold to the touch. Around the stone were five brass cups placed into finely cut divots in the rock slab. In front of each of these brass cups stood a nominee from all corners of our kingdom, each a possible father to my child. In front of everyone, I was disrobed of my silk gown and ushered to the slab where I ceremoniously arranged my naked body. My mother and grandmother took turns reading from the sacred book of prophecy, and while I nervously waited, my eyes wandered the room looking for something to provide a distraction.

My eyes passed over each of the men, looking them up and down, wondering who they were and what kind of child they each might produce. My gaze lingered back to one of them, he looked oddly familiar. He was presented along with several other well decorated warriors and humanitarians who had been recognized the day before in several public ceremonies, celebrating bravery and compassion. Still, there was something about this one man standing before me. I was drawn to the beautiful brown color of his skin, it was a golden brown that glowed with health and self-confidence. He had a very beautiful smile that looked as though it could convince you of anything. His straight dark hair was slicked very tightly back and kept in a braid. I almost did not recognize him until I saw the scar on his face from that day long ago at the Step Well. My heart swelled. Leo had found a way back to me. I caught his eye and he held my gaze. He whispered and asked if any snakes were about to appear, and then made a subtle gesture of a snake slithering with his hand. I laughed and welcomed the break in nervousness and anxiety that had taken over. I loved that he could make me laugh about how awkward this was going to be.

I descended from a matriarchal culture where the leaders were a continuous line of women who were all conceived in a very unconventional method. There was a process of fertilization that was done where the women of the royal line were never touched directly by men. This was to ensure that the Queen would always be a combination of the greatest we had to offer amongst our society. The men who were chosen by their peers presented themselves to the Queen while I lay on the stone slab. The five naked men gathered around me and presented themselves to the Queens. Then, they were expected to fill the brass cup in front of them with their seed. These cups were collected, combined, and then inserted into me using an ancient device that had been used for thousands of years to create our leaders. It was cold and painful at first, but I was so nervous I was able to push the initial shock away. I was made to lay still for quite some time, and when it was over, the men were ushered out of the room. I touched my belly with the hopes that this child has taken root, and another ceremony will not be required.

Later that night Leo woke me from my sleep with a kiss. I do not know how he managed it, but he had come to my quarters. He stayed for many hours, and we both knew he would need to stealthily remove himself before he was seen by anyone. He whispered to me under my silken blankets about how he had managed to work his way back to me, how he planned everyday for the years we were separated to reunite, and how he carefully drugged his own father to get past my guards. He kissed me deeply and promised to come again soon. I tingled at the thought of his return, and then cringed when I saw my mother watching me from her doorway down the corridor. I could tell from the look on her face she had seen Leo leave. She disappeared quietly back into her quarters, unwilling to challenge the break in tradition she had uncovered.

A short time after the impregnation ceremony it was confirmed by our medicine woman that I was indeed a vessel of life. Word was sent out to the furthest corners of Amun, and there was much celebration at the news of my impending child. I fell ill almost immediately after this announcement, and remained nauseated for the duration of the child's growth within me. Leo had managed to convince the Naacals he was needed in Lymuria to help establish the newest wing of their library in the capital. Leo tried as best he could to spend time with me while I adjusted to having a human being inside of me. I was happy to have him there, especially when my body swelled and my face distorted from the pressure of the child. My feet swelled so badly I could not walk or stand on them for more than a few moments at a time. My body ached and I could not find a comfortable position to sit in.

I did not sleep as my dreams were plagued with terrible visions of spiders forming in waves amongst the shadows of my room and enveloping me in their angry march. The smell of many foods made me gag, and despite having excellent cooks to spoil my every need, I did not eat much for many months. Many worried after me during this time, yet none would really leave me in peace. I was grateful to be done with my pregnancy when my labor finally began, and hoped I would never have to repeat such an arduous process.

The sky was strange the night I gave birth. Thunder and lightning shook the palace, but not a single drop of rain fell from the sky. The thunder appeared as green bolts in the sky and zig zagged across the night like the roots of an ancient tree. Some said it was a good omen, but behind my back many said it was a bad omen. No one could understand what it truly was because they had never seen anything like it before. The pressure of the storm was thick around us and the added tension had brought on my labor a few days early. The night air was heavy with moisture and I was drenched in sweat. My mother and grandmother were ushered around the room by the medicine woman and the child reciever.

The future caregiver to my daughter was waiting obediently in the background. She was there to ensure a strict bond between the child and her so she would care for my child as her own. I moved around often and sat in hot tubs of water to ease the child out. When I felt it was time, I squatted while holding on to two ropes that were suspended from the ceiling. Below me were numerous pillows of all shapes and sizes to prevent the slippery newborn from accident or injury. I wore nothing and felt comfortable and free of bodily constraints. My labor was long but mostly painless thanks to the concoctions the medicine woman provided.

On our island grew a white leaf found on a waxy plant that was widely collected. When it was ground down and made into a paste, one could inhale its vapors and be relieved of pain in a very special way. When used during child-birth it allowed for the user to be free of pain but euphorically alert and in tune with the birthing energy. In Amun we had many types of cures for all sorts of ailments that were derived from natural sources one could easily forage. These recipes had been passed down through thousands of years from our ancestors from the stars who planted the most useful variety of medicines on our island. Our schools did much to spread the knowledge of these useful herbs and tinctures so that all who needed them might easily find relief.

It took a little over a day of pushing and panting before my child emerged into the world. I felt like I would burst as I waited for them to announce if I had birthed a daughter or a son. The woman held up a small creature, and I fell in love instantly with the wriggling baby that soon began to wail. The child was quickly checked over and then held by its neck and bottom and presented to my mother. "A daughter has joined us," announced my mother. I was relieved it was a girl, I feared my entire pregnancy I would be the one to break thousands of years of tradition, and now I felt I could finally breathe. My baby was screaming, wailing and I remember them holding her up to me as my mother presented her. She was covered with goo and blood, and screamed so loud her face turned a bright red. I was beyond myself with love and gratitude and overwhelmed with emotion.

My mother handed my baby to my grandmother, who then handed her to me as she said: "This is a new version of you emerging, these are

the cracks that allow for our skin to be shed."
When she handed me my baby, I felt the entire world shift, and never again could remember
what the world felt like before her. This was my
child, my only child, and she would inherit everything. I called her Reo, after my grandmother
Rajini and my best friend Leo.

My mother anointed the baby with a sacred
oil across her forehead, then they wrapped her up
and patched me up with a compress made from
our holistic plants. The child receiver later told
me that my daughter had been born with her eyes
wide open, and that this was a good omen, indeed.
Outside, celebrations went on for days throughout the land of Amun. Fireworks blew through the
sky waking her constantly. As I would rock her
back to sleep, I remember I had never before been
so angry at something so beautiful. I absolutely
loved Reo, and I loved being her mother. I strapped
my newborn baby to me as soon as I recovered
fully from her birth and took her everywhere with
me. The farming families had a system of strapping their babies to them with a mesh netting
they wore around their torso. This was done to
keep the child close to the beating of the mother's
heart while they worked.

This device was a delight for my baby to
be held in, and within moments of strapping her
to me she would fall into a peaceful slumber.
The device did not have the same calming effect
with my mother, who thought this was a crazy,

peasant notion of carrying a child around all day. I was expected to continue my royal duties, and this would require me to leave the baby with her sworn caregiver for long periods of time. I felt this was not necessary, and after some time, the caregiver fell into a deep state of depression on account that I had denied her a job she felt was her reason for being.

Word of this got to my mother who abruptly claimed I was spending too much time with the baby and I needed to start letting others help me. The Queen claimed that delegation was a big part of learning to rule a kingdom, and it started in our personal lives with the things we loved most. We disagreed, and I did as I wanted and took my baby everywhere with me. Some may have found it unprofessional, but I was not in the notion of looking to impress people. I reluctantly performed my duties, and then returned home to the palace to play with my smiling baby.

What only stoked the fire inside my mother was an exuberant Leo showing up in my palace quarters quite often to check in on Reo while he stayed to oversee the new library. He daringly would make lighthearted jokes to my mother about how Reo looked like him. I think we both hoped she was, but we knew there was not a real father in the child's life and there never would be. So much would have to change about who we were to make that possible. I knew there was no way that I could ever abandon my duty to Amun, it wasn't an option. In small ways, I began to push him away because I felt it would not be fair to him to live this type of a life. He loved me very much and I did him, but there was no way of forcing this to work. He wanted us to be a family, and as much as I wanted the same, it was my duty to inform him that we would never, ever be a family.

We each continued to spend time with Reo, sometimes alone, sometimes together. She was growing fast and learning quickly. Before my very eyes she turned from innocent babe into a mischievous gap toothed little spirit, full of fire and life. She first stood up and ran to me before she ever crawled a step. I was astonished in her quick understanding of hand gestures and their linked meanings. Because of our bloodline, the women of my family could recall at a very early age many of the memories of our ancestors. It was interesting to watch her young eyes pick up on her grandmother's growing anxiety. My mother had become deeply agitated because her reign was fast approaching its end, and the great prophecy had not been fulfilled. I felt no sorrow at her loss, but still did not feel enthusiasm about my upcoming ascendancy. I was quickly approaching my reign and in good favor with our people, yet that same despairing feeling from my youth would surface each time I thought of the future.

My Grandmother Rajini taught me many things while my mother Sunisa was commanding the last years of her empire. Foremost, I learned the way to treat my people, and how to relate to them. My grandmother believed a good ruler can not be out of touch with the many layers of her society. There was a heavy sense of duty and sacrifice both my foremothers constantly reminded me of with their long discussions and anecdotes of service. While my mother was more direct and less patient with my lessons, my Grandmother administered great advice on our many beachside walks together. She would constantly remind me during these talks that a good ruler can not hold themselves above their people and expect them to obey just because they are standing above, it was something you must earn, and something you must embody.

Sensing my apprehension, my grandmother wisely advised that it was something you must create within yourself that makes you relatable to your people and allows them to open their hearts to you being their leader. I struggled with this concept. I felt immense anxiety when I envisioned my future as the Queen of Amun, and could not see how the people would want to open their hearts to me. On one of our last beachside walks, I remember my grandmother's final advice to me was "the people want to be led, but they want to be confident in the knowledge that this is the right direction to be led. Do not fail them."

In my child's fourth year I was given a series of ceremonial tattoos reserved for the women of my line. The tattoo was to be one of the few right of passage ceremonies left before I was to begin shadowing my mother in her daily activities to gain perspective on my upcoming position. My ceremonial tattoo was done with sharpened crystals attached to bamboo poles that were repetitively tapped into my skin. Different colored inks derived from natural sources from all corners of our kingdom were used to show the unification of Amun. On my back, the tattoo was an elaborate piece that featured a large circle with a grounded woman to one side and a floating man to the other. Within the circle was the symbol XX, which was from our earliest ancient language and meant "where there is will, there is a way."

While the tattoo was done, the head of the Naacal Brotherhood recited the ancestral prayer dedicated to the celestial born father of Queen Oona, the first leader of Amun: "Oh Father of the sky, sacred be your name. Your day will come, your will be done, on our earthly home Amun. Give us this, your wisdom and guidance and forgive us our failings. Guide us and deliver us on our earthly mission."

It takes what feels like many hours of repetitive flashing pain before I begin to enter a trance-like state where I can float above the discomfort. Even though it was a lengthy process, I knew there would be no rest for me after this ritual. Lymuria would be hosting many events that evening in celebration of a comet's return to our night sky that had not been seen since my grandmother was a child. There would be many ceremonies and celebrations to attend and many dignitaries to converse with, so I prepared myself for a long evening without my daughter Reo.

After the painful tattoo was complete, I had returned to my room to try to lull my sweet Reo to sleep. Something was not right about her though. She cried and cried, and I held her and walked through the room, but this did nothing to satisfy her. Despite the pain her weight brought to my sore tattoo, I continued to carry her and walked out onto my private patio that faced out onto the ocean.

My child wailed louder as I limped out into the eerie stillness that had descended onto my private beachfront. I sang softly in her ear to calm her, but my child began to wail hysterically. I grew frustrated and turned and faced the night sky. At the horizon in the distance floated 6 large orbs in the sky. The orbs glowed green in the sky amongst the vividly pink backdrop of the setting sun. My insides grew cold and retracted inward as I pulled my child tightly to my chest. My toes begin to curl from the uncomfortable energy coursing through my veins. My daughter was now screaming inconsolably, and inside, I was screaming. I did not understand what I saw and I was suddenly afraid. I felt sick inside and could not shake the feeling that the orbs have come for me specifically.

In the distance, I could hear the brass warning bell ringing from within the capitol. Within a few moments of this ancient alarm sounding, my daughter and I were surrounded by my guards who began to move us inside the palace, away from the unsettling floating orbs. A heavy mist had begun to settle on our skins in the deep stillness of the stagnant evening heat. The mist distorted the orbs and made them blurry glowing blobs in the dusk sky.

My sobbing child gasped for breath as we were hurried by my guards into the palace's stone clad room of defense, and waited there impatiently until my mother and grandmother arrived a few moments later. My grandmother looked pale and shaken, but my mother, I had never seen her look so happy in all my life. The Queen was exhilarated and fervently announced that we must prepare for our guests' arrival. The prophecy had begun.

PART TWO

THE OTHERS

THE OTHERS

His name was Osiris and he was their leader. Along with five of his best men he had traveled from afar in search of a cure for a virus that was devastating their land, an island they called Atlantis. They were tall and very pale, as if they had not seen the sun for quite some time. Their mouths and noses were covered by a tight fitting black mask that formed to the curve of their face. The Others had dark circles under their eyes and smelled of desperation. They came seeking knowledge, they needed to know about the healing power that surrounded our island. For nearly two years a mysterious virus had held their society hostage and killed the masses without discrimination. They were desperate for a cure, and so my mother welcomed them into our home so they may sit with us and find guidance from the other realm.

We tried to explain to them that we did not have the ability to share the healing powers that enveloped the land of Amun. My people had a miraculous ability to maintain good health- it was due to a protective system of energy that stretched across our island and bounced off the water's edge. There were always injuries, births, and deaths in our land, but never disease or imbalances of the body. It was a gift that had been given to us by our ancestors from the stars when they landed here and installed the healing technology into our island's framework.

We reiterated that it was a gift, and not something we could give. We could not extend the healing energy to our overseas colonies as well, and this point was brought to their attention by my Grandmother. The Others would not take this answer even though we tried many times to explain. They did not feel that we were being honest about our inability to share this immunity, and their leader Osiris grew impatient with us. Time could not be wasted, he needed a cure and he needed it to be portable. My mother assured him we would consult the ancestors in meditation and find an answer.

When they first arrived, I was very confused as to why my people were so trusting of the Others, so enamored by their presence. I could not understand why my mother was so undoubting of the Atlantean visitors and their motives. It seemed so obvious to me that they were up to something disturbing. Even so, my mother blindly believed that this was a foretold time when our ancient ancestors would be reunited and we would merge our powers together, a true fulfillment of destiny during her reign. Deep inside I knew this was a pivotal point in our existence, but I felt strangely off about the whole thing.

The Others seemed to have watched us for a while, and that sat unwell with me. They knew of our names, our many towns and attractions, they even remarked on bits of our history. My mother was delighted in these anecdotes but I was more interested in understanding how they knew so much, yet we knew so little of them. Bothered by this, I asked my grandmother "why take so long to announce yourself if we were destined to be reunited?" My heart sank as she frowned and told me to stop looking so hard at everything.

It was under my grandmother's tutelage that I had studied our legends closely. The information was passed down that there had been others like our ancestors who had left the home planet and were sprinkled around the Earth into colonies. We understood that one day there was an inevitable destiny of us being reunited with the other colonies for mutually beneficial growth. It was believed a leap in our existence would occur upon our reunification.

In fairness to my mother, they did fit the description of lore I knew so well, and their technology rang with similarity to our earlier ancestor's tools. Even so, I was unable to remove the feeling that something was not right about the situation. I had a cold twisting feeling inside when I met them. It was the same feeling I experienced when I opened the leaky wooden door I encountered as a child, and saw the water rush.

Osiris and the Others made me weary. Despite my previous insistence to keep Reo in my care at all times, I instead made the choice to leave her in my quarters at the palace with her caregiver, along with several guards. How quickly I traded in my steadfast beliefs when it came to a gut instinct about the safety of my child. Looking to protect her in all ways I could, I made a point to question them and inquire about their history. The Others sparingly offered me bits and pieces of a story detailing a far-off island nation that they painted as having greatly advanced technology and a highly evolved society.

Osiris claimed Atlantis was nearly on the other side of the world, in a different ocean than ours. Their preferred mode of travel was a real marvel to behold, and charmed all who approached the other worldly iridescent spheres that travelled silently through the air like lightning. Amongst the others there were no women, only men. All six of the others had full heads of hair that matched the silvery blonde streak the women of my line all possessed. Osiris claimed their hair color was because they were all descendents of the ancient founder of Atlantis, a visitor to Earth called Atlas.

The timing of their quest was perfect, as we were able to hold a strong ceremony of meditative travel with the full moon that accompanied their arrival. In the late evening when the moon was high in the night sky, we led Osiris to a special room in the center of the palace to join in consulting the ancestors. This was the room where we housed our collection of the sacred Red Crystals. My mother concocted a special drink from muddling a particular purple root grown in the sacred garden with fresh water from the spring of the Divine Mother Evi.

Traditionally, the drink would be taken first by the person who created it, and then passed to others participating. Only a few small sips are necessary to feel its heavy effects. It was quite easy to slip into trance with the help of the mixture. All else around us faded away slowly as the Red Crystals were unveiled on their intricately cut stone altar. I saw the eyes of Osiris widen in disbelief at the crystals as my grandmother approached the largest one and proudly carried it back to our meditative platform. She placed it in the middle of our huddle and we ceremoniously grabbed each other by the wrists, and closed our eyes. When the right tone was created by striking one of our brass bowls, you would feel a tingling sensation begin in your scalp, which would carry itself down the spine to the toes. The feeling would allow for the body to relax enough so it may begin to mentally travel and seek the answers you require.

If done correctly a wormhole will open up and you can travel free beyond your body, beyond yourself. You can see the entirety of the Universe and feel the warmth of a mother's womb. It was a strange feeling of encapsulation that brought on a deep paralysis of the body. You may not understand the answers they show at first, but they always make sense to the seer within time. Depending on the Red Crystal that was used, there will be certain information stored within meant specifically for the situation at hand.

On this night we had chosen to use a special crystal, one that was rarely used. It was a powerful gem that carried many secrets of our origins that my line had yet to unlock. My mother had an affinity towards this large Red Crystal pillar and thought it might help to have the extra energy of Osiris in awakening this crystal bound memory. I involved him in our ceremony only at my mother's request to help them find a cure for their virus. I made a mistake when I did that, I showed our power to the wrong people. Our minds opened together as one, and from somewhere within the endless bounds of the Universe, the story of our origin reached out through this Red Crystal and began to embed itself into our minds.

It was a long journey to Earth, and my crew and I were eager to arrive and begin our colonization mission. Our home planet's resources had dwindled to unreliable levels, and it was in our best interest to find a backup planet for when the day would come that our planet would die. When we found Earth, we knew we had found something special. Our people had evolved so deeply that we truly did not feel an array of emotions. When we first saw Earth, it sparked within us something that could not be left alone. It was what we had been waiting for, and in time, would help us fulfill our next evolutionary step. Many generations before me had initiated the beginnings of the human experiment, and now it was time to move them to the next level by creating a hybrid child of our mixed blood. As Commander of the ship, it was my mission to see through to the end a successful integration of both our species to ensure dual survival.

We traveled on an advanced ship through a wormhole to the galaxy that held the seedling outpost we called Earth. As we entered Earth's atmosphere there suddenly were several small explosions on board my ship. I heard an alarm sound as the monitors showed the air quality was decreasing and systems were failing. I commanded the crew to brace for impact as we crashed into dark water and the ship embedded into a rock wall. There we suddenly stopped and hung in place as water dripped around us slowly filling up the ship's cabin. Of the seven members in my exploration crew, two died on impact. I saw the way their necks dangled from their torsos and instantly knew they were gone. It felt like slow motion as I looked around the half flooded ship and saw the remaining four crew were injured but alive. We needed to get out before the water got any higher. I gripped the exit latch swiftly, and told them all to brace for water. The door lifted into the ship and my crew and I were sucked into the swell. The five of us burst to the surface of the water within seconds of each other, confused, cold, and wet. It was like being ripped from a womb, and while gasping for your first breath, being thrown into a frozen world filled with panic.

My remaining crew successfully launched their flotation mechanisms within their jumpsuits and floated to the rocky shoreline. The blue jumpsuit I wore had ripped during the landing and filled with a sudden burst of cold water that made me feel numb and heavy. The ripped suit did not expand for flotation, but I was lucky enough to grab onto a piece of floating debris from the ship and kicked heavily to shore as quickly as I could. We all sat on the icy rock ledge for a small eternity, not knowing what to do. My shivering was overwhelming, so I began to jump up and down to try and stop my body from freezing. The dark segmented rock that surrounded us made everything feel colder. I was told it would be colder than on our planet, but I was not prepared for this. My crew soon followed and began to jump around me, waking up their frozen limbs. Then, we began to briskly walk so we would not die from exposure, and so we walked all night and into the daylight hours.

I will never forget the feeling I had in my stomach as I led my crew into the night. There was this hunger coming from right in the pit of my stomach. It felt like it was dying, like it must eat, it must have something to suck from. It felt like there was something in there that was pulling me downward from an otherworldly place. This was my first journey to this *planet, and my first human body. I had not known hunger before Earth, and it was terrifying to experience it for the first time. For so long there was no need to eat where we came from. I did not truly understand the concept of eating when I was trained for my mission. My crew and I trained extensively for the adaptation that would happen to our bodies when we landed. We had many tools that were meant to help us easily transition and protect us in the interim until we could build permanent structures. All of those adaptive technologies we abandoned on the ship as we bailed out and swam for our lives. We had nothing, and no choice but to keep moving or die. I trudged forward following a stream of water, not entirely sure how much longer my nearly frozen crew would continue to follow behind their commander.*

In the shaded distance, it appeared that a large, hairy beast was approaching us from the evergreen thicket. I prepared to fight off the animal to give my crew the chance to flee for what remained of their lives. The animal stood a short distance away and lingered, not moving forward, just watching us. Suddenly, it exhaled a cloud of smoke and its paws threw off the layer of fur it wore over its head. A human woman stared back at me, her crudely sewn animal furs keeping her insulated and comfortable in the frigid elements that surrounded us. I staggered towards her and fell to my knees in frozen exhaustion. Mercifully, she pointed in a direction and we followed her through the thicket. She took us back to the cave she shared with her small clan. Around the fire in their cave, my crew sat and started to defrost while the sinking reality of what had happened to us began to settle in. From a woven basket hidden in a far corner of her cave, Evi produced spherical fruit that was red and yellow in color. I bit into it and my mouth was filled with such taste that I cried tears of joy with each bite.

I was a bit dazed as I looked at the array of faces joined together around the burning fire in the cave. Amongst my crew, we were similar looking, with silvery blond hair, tall bodies, and bright colored almond shaped eyes on elongated faces. Our tight fitting blue jumpsuits all carried a badge on the chest that depicted a crescent moon alongside three other moons of varying sizes. This was the badge of our planet's exploration program, a collection of selected individuals chosen to find planets where life could be sustained and begin the seeding process.

Around the fire, the humans stared at us with wide eyes full of wonder. They were much shorter and stouter than us, with masses of dark curly hair covering their heads, faces, and bodies. I found it striking just how different our seedlings on Earth physically compared to our original design. Our mission was to enlighten them with our technology, and genetically perfect them so that we may interbreed and continue our species existence. Our skin could not tolerate the sun's ultraviolet rays on Earth, and this was the only way to ensure our species survival. We had suits to protect us, but that would not work in the long run. It would take thousands of years for our natural offspring to evolve to tolerate the sun, and we did not *have time for that. It was our goal to ensure that a successful hybrid child would be born, and with this ensure our species continuation.*

My crew and I lived in the cave with the clan for quite some time. Evi, the young woman who had delivered us from death, used a basic form of sign language to communicate and instruct on the habits of their survival. Evi and her clan used primitive medicine and knowledge of earthly plants to heal our wounds and fill our stomachs. We assisted in their daily chores and made ourselves useful, though none of us felt quite that useful without our technology. My second in command, his name was Atlas. He was the first one of my crew to suggest that we try to reclaim the lost technology, and believed we should trek back to the crash site when warm weather arrived to salvage what was left. I was not sure it would be safe for any member of the crew to re-enter the ship, and assumed the water had corroded much, if not all inside. Atlas had difficulty adjusting to the new path of our mission after our crash landing. He was one that needed to feel of great importance to others, and so he persisted in making plans to retrieve our machinery. I knew it would take some time for the weather to improve, so I agreed with Atlas on the recovery mission and continued to learn what I could from Evi and her clan.

The day finally arrived when the warm weather settled in and we began our journey back to the crash site with Evi leading the way. One of the things we needed most was a dull blood red gemstone that was found within a crumbling silver colored dirt throughout the Universe. We would use this gemstone to regulate our bodies while transferring energy when using our technology; without them, our technology was useless. For the beholder, the Red Crystals control the future and the past, as they hold many roles in our history and continue to influence our future. There was within these gems the ability to build empires and annihilate entire civilizations, should the conditions of our experiment require so. On our home planet we had exhausted our deposits of the Red Crystals. Unfortunately, there is no way to create these powerful Red Crystals, you could only be lucky enough to cross paths with one.

When we arrived at the crash site you could hardly tell such a major event had happened here not so long ago. The ship was stuck many feet below the surface and the water's darkness hid its secrets well. The rocky area was still quite chilled despite the heat, and the second I jumped in I felt the same cold panic I experienced during our rough landing. I noticed a similar shock has taken over some of my crew members as they tepidly dipped into the water. The frigid water did not phase Atlas. He swam with quick precision under the shadowy water into the craft, and began surfacing with various items from the wreckage. The other crew members formed a chain and unloaded the contents onto the hard rock that lined the water's edge. Atlas showed great determination as he labored in his task. I knew what was driving him, it was his desire to distance himself away from the clan.

I noticed the dynamic between Atlas and the humans had changed since we arrived. He had little tolerance for the people of Evi's clan and treated them terribly. The clan grew anxious from his demeaning attitude and avoided his gaze. I had tried to reason with Atlas and remind him that the clan had saved our lives, and he still insisted we move on from this clan and search for another to experiment with. I had not seen this side of my crewmate before our journey, and wondered how he could transition to such an opinion so quickly. I knew his head had been injured in the crash, and often felt this had been the instigation for his personality change. I could feel him breaking away from our crew and despite how I had previously felt, I was now relieved for the welcome change in routine with our trip back to the crash site.

We continued to dive to the ship and brought up many things that could be of use, though most of the technology was corroded and would need extensive repairs. Our numerous trips underwater had still not located the Red Crystals, so we persisted despite the cold. At one point, I went back up for air, but Atlas did not follow. I worried he was possibly caught on something and trapped in the craft. I sucked in my breath and went under again. I started panicking when I could not find Atlas. My breath was nearly gone and I needed to resurface. I looked one last time for him and felt immense relief as I saw Atlas shoot up from below me. In his arms were the Red Crystals we needed so greatly, he had so many of them in his hands I feared he would drop some. We propelled up to the surface and

I assisted him with swimming the crystals to shore. As we dried by Evi's fire, the crew examined what we had salvaged, and were surprised to find several pieces of our mobile equipment still working despite the submersion. For the first time in months Atlas and my crew looked truly happy, and I felt what I believed was hope begin to uplift us all on our journey back to the cave.

Our priorities differed as my crew and I returned to the clan with our salvaged bounty. I felt we should build an altar to the Divine Universe with the Red Crystals. When built and arranged properly on top of a rift in the Earth's energy, its powers can be used to contact the home planet briefly. My goal was to try and communicate our crash landing to them and let them know we planned to continue to experiment using what we had at hand. Atlas did not think we needed to notify them, I believe he felt great shame over our crash landing and failure to begin our earthly experiment. Atlas instead took a crystal from my altar to use a salvaged device that melted and molded stone, and then informed us that he was leaving to go live by himself. With one of the handheld devices, Atlas melted and levitated a new home for himself from the large stones near our settlement. I tried my best to communicate with the home planet, but my altar was too weak, and I dejectedly disbanded it and distributed the crystals to my crew so they may begin their work.

Of all the problems we faced during our first year on Earth, I was blessed to find a willing participant for our great experiment in Evi. Through the course of our exchange she had communicated using the sign language we had developed that she wanted a child, but did not want a mate. This was uncommon for her clan, as a mate was security for the infant's survival, but not an unheard of action. Evi was a leader of her clan, and amongst her people she was not looked down upon for her participation in our experiment. Her people loved her and trusted her judgement. I began using rudimentary artificial insemination methods on her to spur the life of a hybrid child. Sadly, most of her impregnantions would end within a few weeks of implantation. Even so, she was willing to continue to experiment with me despite the physical and mental toll of such continued loss. Over time, something unplanned began to happen in our experiment. I noticed Evi grew more aware with each of her pregnancies, as if the fetus was somehow imparting its otherworldly genetic wisdom onto her. There were six tries I attempted over time with our implantation technology. Every pregnancy ended the same way. Evi never saw her stomach swell and I know this weighed heavy on her. Over time, the loss of the children brings us closer. We can feel something between us, something that draws us together. She has trouble pronouncing the name my crew calls me, Commander Attoms, so she called me Adom, a word unfamiliar to her before our meeting.

During the course of my time working with Evi, my crew had been productive building new accommodation for themselves and the clan. They had melted and levitated large blocks quarried from a nearby source and created many stone structures with small openings in the front for easy access. The tightly fit stone offered waterproofing for my crew and their equipment. Over time, they built more of these mega-lithic homes for the clan, and began to proceed with plans for building an aqueduct system. Cassian and Orion were my two crew members most dedicated to this art. They spent countless hours toiling over design and angle, even arguing over placement down to the last detail. The technology they used was very powerful and not for amateurs. One wrong move and you could easily blow yourself or another into a thousand tiny shards of blood and bone.

Cassian and Orion had grown very attached during their time on Earth. While I often heard them argue over the details of their work, their disagreements were always solved quickly, usually with Orion having the final say in the matter. Then came the day Cassian had the final say. It was late in the evening after a hot day of melting and maneuvering stone. From the work site you could hear their arguing grow louder and more heated. As I approached the commotion, I could hear a vile zapping sound followed by a sickeningly distinct splatter. I found Cassian alone, holding the stone melting device, shaking in fear and covered in blood. He claimed it had been a power struggle for the device to control who would make the proper cut in the stone they were working on, neither had meant to hurt each other. He swore it was an accident, he did not mean to hurt his friend. Cassian claimed the trigger accidentally went off as they fought over the device like children. I wanted to believe him, but his behavior after the incident became erratic and distant. He would no longer join us or converse about the mission. Cassian isolated himself and could be heard arguing with someone in his vacant quarters. I'm not sure if it was guilt or regret, but it was not long before Cassian used the same stone melting device on himself. It was not long after Orion's death that we found Cassians remains painting the walls inside the stone cube he had crafted as his living quarters.

The last crew member to remain with the clan and I was Iona. During my work with Evi, Iona had been my assistant on the implantation procedures. After the many failures, Iona offered herself up as host for a human hybrid child. There were many reasons why I believed it would not work, foremost that it would be too dangerous without the proper medical equipment. Our bodies and heads were narrower, and I was sure a newborn human head would not find passage without detriment to both the mother and child. Iona was a steadfast believer in the mission and was adamant that we proceed with the implantation. Evi and I watched in wonder as Iona's stomach grew with life over the next few months. Evi once again chose to try the implantation process, I believe it was the influence of Iona's pregnancy that rekindled in her that desire to bring life into the world. It once again was successful for Evi, and for a short period of time we were blissful in the anticipation of two new beings that will be the first of their kind in our new world.

I knew I could not hold on to the magnificence of that feeling, for within a few days Evi once again miscarried, and this time set off into the wild to find solace in her isolation. This upset Iona so greatly that she went into premature labor and struggled for days to push out a poorly formed hybrid that I was sure would not survive its passage. As I had regretfully predicted, the child's head was stuck in Iona's narrow pelvis. After watching her suffer for what felt like eternity, finally I had to do it, I cut her, and within moments the child was born. It was a tiny boy who showed signs of malformity. The child wailed weakly and made small guttural noises that did not sound promising. Iona held her child as I worked to stem the bleeding with the tools from the ship that still functioned.

Iona screamed that the baby was not breathing, and her bleeding worsened in her hysteria. Iona bled out and died holding her grey child tightly to her breast. I do not remember how long it was until Evi returned and found me with the rigid bodies of Iona and her child. We buried them in each other arms, to spend eternity entangled together...it was the least we could do. Time blurred for me for some time, but Evi did not leave my side during my grief. She had become my mate in all this misery, my other half from another world. I was overjoyed and terrified when Evi told me one night in our sign language that she was again pregnant with my child.

The last member of my crew left alive with me was Atlas. I went to him and despite our history together, I begged him for help. I needed another to assist in Evi's delivery, I could not let what happened to Iona happen once more. I could not lose Evi, she was all I had. Despite my belief her pregnancy would end just as all the others did, this child had chosen to grow, thrive in fact. We were close to delivery, and I felt insecure from my previous failure. Atlas did not respond as I hoped he would. He was in favor of taking the Red Crystals and going through a Chasm in search of others like us. I could not agree, the Chasm was no place for a woman about to give birth, it was too unpredictable.

The Chasm was created by the earliest visitors from my home planet. It was meant to transport us from a seedling community if the need should arise to abandon the experiment. The opening of a Chasm was found within a megalithic stone circle positioned specifically to ensure the right amount of exposure to wind and light for the Chasm's vortex to operate. The Chasm would transport you to another stone circle opening, but you could never be sure where you would end up, the Chasm chose where to send you based on your energy and its vibrational match within the Earth. During our training for our mission, we had been warned to not put humans through the Chasm, it provoked something within their brains and evolved them too quickly.

Atlas had spent his days of isolation secretly building a Chasm and proudly shared confirmation of its existence. He countered my cry for help with a fresh start. When I refused to leave with him for the *last time, Atlas claimed he was done with our experiment and would be leaving alone with the Red Crystals. "Come find me when you are ready to go home," he screamed at me. We argued and lashed out years worth of resentments at each other. Then, in a moment of rage he threatened to use the Red Crystals to reset the experiment if Evi's labor was not successful. I believed him when he threatened to reset everything; he despised the clan and had never been fond of Evi. A reset from the power of the Red Crystal would undoubtedly mean death for the humans and myself. I did my best to hide this information from Evi, but she had become very intuitive as a result of her latest pregnancy. She perceptively felt the creeping doom enveloping her clan, and made a decision one night while I slept to save her people in the event her delivery was not successful.*

When I woke that terrible morning, she was gone. I searched for Evi frantically. I had no idea where she had gone, and looked high and low throughout our community. I ran to find Atlas, but his stone cube was empty, the salvaged technology he claimed was gone. My frantic search for Evi became erratic. I alerted the clan and caused a panic amongst them. Search parties were sent out to look for Evi, but returned with no trace of her. I believed the unthinkable had happened to my mate and child. I searched for weeks until I exhausted myself into a neglected state. Riddled with grief and failure, I crawled into a cave behind a spray of giant ferns and died there alone.

What I have learned since departing my earthly

body was that Evi had unknowingly found herself in the Chasm with the Red Crystals during the perfect moment for transport. Her otherworldly fetus controlled her instinct and guided her to the swirling Chasm inside the stone circle just as Atlas was about to use it to leave for good. The two were sucked in simultaneously and sent to opposite ends of the Earth. Evi was transported to a stone circle of megalithic statues with carved faces, and discovered by another group from my planet that had also crash landed. Their spacecraft was not as damaged as ours had been, and nearly all their technology was salvageable. Thankfully, this includes all the medical equipment needed to safely bring my child into this Universe.

Evi had been injured in her transport through the Chasm, and the child inside began to distress. On a large stone slab they placed Evi while they used their equipment to painlessly remove the child through an incision in her womb that was burned shut once the child was lifted out. They cared for both mother and child and gave them quarters amongst their people. This community my lucky daughter was born into were a joyful group who instilled a deep appreciation of compassion and fairness into their culture. Evi called my daughter Oona, and her descendents were the leaders of millions.

As for Atlas and his journey through the Chasm, my crewmate found himself propelled to a stone circle on an island he later named Atlantis. The original colonizers to this stone circle failed in their experiment and had vanished at some point before his arrival. Atlas quickly captured and experimented on the humans who inhabited the island. His work was careful and deliberate, and before long he created an entire race in his image. With the technology left-over from the vanished colonists, he became a God to them as he could easily create in ways that operated beyond their comprehension. The people of Atlantis worshipped him as the Lord of the Sea, as he painted himself as a savior from the water who liberated them from their blinding ignorance. Over time, his island became very advanced, and was heavily constructed to create a replica of what we had left behind on the home planet.

I have placed this memory here to show you the origins of our people come from a place of love. Our goal was to bring all of our colonies together and continue our eternal evolution here on this planet, in a society that promoted equality amongst its inhabit-ants to ensure a mutually sustained survival. When I first took on my mission, I could not foresee how things would unfold and looking back, I wish I had acted differently on many occasions. I do not know if this would have made a difference in our experiments outcome, but what I do know is that it was imperative that we should be here and that we should be continu-ing this great experiment. The Universe is unfolding as it should be. Trust that it will guide you in your journey.

We met again with the Others the next day. They were unsatisfied with our session and re-

quired additional answers in their quest for an
end to the virus that plagued their society. Osiris wanted to know more about our Red Crystals,
how we used them and then surprisingly, where
we kept them. I noticed they now each wore a
device strapped to a belt on their waists. It was
rectangular and made of a type of dark grey metal
I had never seen before. I know my mother and
grandmother noticed their devices immediately
as well because I could feel a shift in the room
that began to feel uncomfortable. "What are those
for?" questioned my grandmother with slitted
eyes. But before they could answer my mother
interjected and insisted we would go back to consult the ancestors to find answers to end their
plague.

My mother was very diplomatic, she did
not want to offend Osiris. She believed in the
prophecy, but still, she knew she lacked information on the Others. A secret decree was issued
immediately after this in which Queen Sunisa
sent messengers out from all corners of Amun and
into the colonies to send scouts from each region
to uncover any detail they could on the Others.
Thousands set off in groups of three from each village and outpost. Word was to be sent back immediately with any information that could serve
useful to the Queen.

Leo came to my quarters later that night,
I woke to find him standing over my daughter,

watching her dream. He told me he must leave to go on a mission for my mother under the guise of the Naacal Brotherhood. They have ordered him to take secret documents to a new outpost that some informants believe might be close to the Island of Atlantis. He said he would return as soon as possible, and hoped I would reconsider his plan to live together as a family. I became abruptly irate with him, and his assumption that I had a choice in any of this. I avoided his gaze and piercingly told him what he did not want to hear: "We both know we will never be a family." Without responding, Leo kissed my sleeping child's head, turned from me, and left into the darkness without ever looking back. I would live to regret those cutting words in ways I could never imagine.

Early the next morning I reluctantly left a sleeping Reo with her caregiver and guards to join my matriarchs for a private session with the Red Crystals. During our meditative journey the message from our ancestors was clear, we were not to give them the Red Crystals. My spirit guide Oona explained to me that the illness is something they must go through as a society in order to reach the next stage of evolution, and deterrence from this path would leave them in a stagnant state. I appealed to Oona that we must have an answer to this, too many will die if we leave it unaided. Oona dissipated before my eyes and I knew they would tell us no more. When we returned to the great hall of the palace, the Others had arrived and grew impatient with our absence.

My mother was quick to smooth things over with them and shared that even though we cannot communicate a cure, we were willing to give them one of our Red Crystals as a show of good faith in bridging our nations. Osiris looked insulted when he saw the small Red Crystal my mother presented. He coldly thanked us and said he must depart for the day to test the crystal. I was at a loss for words with my mother. I believed she had gone mad and confronted her about her actions as soon as we could be alone. She assured me that I must trust her, that she knows what is best for us or she would not have been chosen to lead during this time.

For most of my life the Red Crystals were held at the palace in a special room designed to foster the perfect conditions of wind, water, and sunlight they require to charge properly for our sessions. Once though, when I was much younger, I was taken by my mother to a special cave that was very difficult to get to. Surrounded by a quadrant of enormous volcanic rocks spewed out from the sea stood a lonely island vertically jutting out into the sky. On the very top there was a cave that discreetly had an opening wide enough to let in rain, wind and sunlight to charge the crystals if they needed to be stored away. When I helped my mother arrange the crystals at the stone altar there as a child, you could hear a slight sizzle in the air that made my toes tingle and my arm hairs stand up on end.

The cave was the design of our earliest ancestors, and knowledge of its entry was something sworn to secrecy by the few who knew of its existence. The Cave of the Red Crystals was our last resort to save our most precious resource. I was relieved to find out from my grandmother that my mother had sent two of her guards to the cave and hid away the rest of our crystals before giving Osiris his gift.

We knew Orisris and the Others would be back, but none could imagine what he returned to the palace with. A few days later he stood before us and in his hands gleaned the triangular device our ancient ancestors had used to melt and maneuver stone. Perfectly fit into a small crevice on top of the stone melting device was the Red Crystal my mother had given him. I was shocked to see Osiris and his men had removed their masks for the first time since arriving. They looked smug and very much like they were done playing political games with us. In place of the Atlantean uniform we had grown accustomed to seeing them wear, Osiris and his men instead wore sleek jumpsuits that looked like they were made of liquid metal. I had never seen such a quality to any material before that. On their waists again hung the menacing rectangles. It looked like they were preparing to go into battle.

I was filled with anxiety as I quietly studied their new attire, wondering why they would have presented themselves this way and what was their plan. "You have shown us much hospitality and graciousness in our search for a cure to the virus that plagues my people", said Osiris, "Our study of the Red Crystal you provided shows great promise in directing us to a cure for this contagion. We would like to continue its study on our island and will require the remainder of your collection to do so." My mother stared back with a knowing smile on her face, unfazed by his request. "The Red Crystals will not be leaving Amun," my mother proclaimed in a loud clear voice that rallied within me something deep and fierce. Our guards stood taller and their muscles tensed as they waited for word to pounce.

Osiris was undaunted by my mother's response. "In that case, before we depart each other's company" he held up the ancient device and its embedded Red Crystal, "I would like to thank you for returning to us the one Red Crystal, we have found excellent use for it." And in the blink of an eye, he aimed the device at my mother and activated it before her guards could lift their staffs. The beam of light that shot out of the device felt like it moved in slow motion as it hit my mother's abdomen and shattered her into a wet red mush that covered everyone in the room. I wanted to look away, but I could not.

In that instant I felt her rip away from us. The Others wasted not a second in using their rectangular devices and created a wave of energy that caused the rest of us to fall to the floor and convulse. We gagged for breath and rolled around in the bloody bits of my mother while they searched the palace for the crystals. When they failed to locate the Red Crystals, Osiris returned and lingered above my convulsing body as I struggled to breathe he said "the next time I see you it will be your people's blood you are bathed in."

There was no need to doubt Osiris, I understood the threat and knew I needed to take action. After they left we were slowly able to regain our footing and pull ourselves from the blood soaked floor. My grandmother and I were brought to the safe room Reo was being kept in. I wanted to hold my baby, but was covered in blood. Her caregiver tried to pull my screaming child away from me, but Reo ripped free and jumped into my arms, covering herself in my mother's blood. I don't know how long I sat there holding her, rocking into oblivion. My grandmother sat across from me shivering, her face grey and her eyes staring at the ground intensely. There was nothing I could do or say to fix this.

I felt powerless, and then at the same time, realized I was now the Queen of Amun. I always felt that I could never be as good of a leader as my Mother was. She was a perfect leader, just and brave, and now she was gone. One of the most important things that she taught me was to be able to look at something terrifying and to be brave in its face, to hold my head up and to never shrink to it's overwhelming strength above you. Her motherly instinct to impart this lesson would serve me until my dying day.

Word of Queen Sunisa's death spread quickly. Amun was now on high alert and any sign of the Others was to be reported and their trespassing halted. We truly did not have time to process my mother's death because the coronation ceremony needed to be held right away. The people of Amun needed a ruler now more than ever, and it was my responsibility to see them through this uncertainty. Plans were hastily made through the night, and with the first light of morning the coronation would begin and my fate would be solidified.

I recalled from my mother's coronation that there was a tradition of leaving the palace in the darkness of the morning and traveling by foot to the nearby monastery of the Naacal Brotherhood. After we knocked three times using the brass knockers that adorned the large wooden doors, they silently greeted us and ushered us into the structure.

When I arrived with my grandmother and daughter, the Nacaals solemnly led us to the atrium found within the center of the large structure they inhabited. Above me was a stained glass ceiling that had a geometric flower of life pattern that was identical to the one found in our palace. It was dark upon our arrival, but as the ceremony began, the sun rose and changed the energy of the room. The bright pink and yellow rays of the dawn cascaded radiantly from above and created a prismatic show of iridescent light that bounced off the ultra white walls. Below this glassed dome I was lifted above all others onto a stone cube platform in the center of the room.

Around me I was encircled by the thousands that could fit inside, while hundreds of thousands had gathered around the building and piled into the streets for as far as the eye could see. The gown I wore was mostly metal beadwork and in this crowded room it felt like it was cooking me alive. The sunlight gained in force and the pressure of the situation weighed down heavily. I stood as still as I could manage on top of the stone cube, I was too afraid to move, even breathe. There was a heavy crown that I wore made from a metal that was melted down from the ancient technology brought from the stars. The center of my crown held a multifaceted crystal which caused it to tip forward with any sudden movements. I had to hold my head very far back with my nose up in the air in order to keep the crown balanced on my head. My neck ached and cramped from the crown's weight, but it was not an option to remove it, or it will be seen as a bad omen.

As I gazed out at my people, my insecurities melted away and I found myself in a very vengeful mood. I still had my mother's dried blood under my nails, and I was hungry to take action as a leader. My instinct was to irrationally do damage to Osiris and the Others for what they have done to my mother, but I knew we had to complete the coronation first in order to legitimize my warring actions against them. We had never before in Amun faced such a threat or such uncertainty, and I was ready to act in violent ways that only a short time ago I would have rejected.

My terrible thoughts paused as my tiny daughter came forward through the crowd struggling to carry the rounded scepter that was nearly as big as her own head. The scepter's golden sheen reflected bright flashes of light from the domed window above that burned into my eyes and caused them to water.

Behind Reo was my grandmother, Queen Rajini with the royal staff in hand, a golden column with ridges along the sides that mimicked the grand columns that marked the island of Amun. During the coronation of my mother, I remember my grandmother explained that the staff was symbolic of a good leader, "it is who has control, not who has the biggest staff," she told me. The scepter was to remind the new leader that her peoples world was in her hands, and it was to be held carefully and with esteem. Reo kneeled and presented me the sphere, and as she leaned to hand it to me I remembered giving this to my mother at her coronation and watching my grandmother present her the staff. It must have hurt my grandmother a lot to have to hand it to me, but she managed to keep her face rock solid as she placed the staff in my hands.

The room darkened as the staff was placed in my hand, and thunder rumbled heavily in the distance. My daughter had a fear of thunder and looked frightened as she moved closer to my grandmother. Her tiny crown began to slide off her head, but my grandmother put it back in place and straightened my child instead of embracing her. Through the domed window above me were wavy shades of grey darkening in color as they moved like a river across the sky. The head of the Nacaals presented my grandmother with the sacred oil to anoint my forehead. She cried silently as she used her finger to draw a seven sided star with the sacred oil on my forehead.

The wind suddenly picked up and ushered in the darkest clouds I had ever seen. The glass dome protected me from the threatening onslaught of water, but for the hundreds of thousands who stood gathered around outside, rain was an inevitable fate. The masses were quietly stunned at first, but as the first drops fell, all out panic ensued. Many began to push and shove their way to covered areas as a torrential downpour cascaded down in sheets. Scores of people were trampled and left with broken bones and bloody wounds that needed stitching. The deluge showed no signs of letting up, and so masses of spectators left for their homes in the watery onslaught.

Traditionally, there would have been three days of dancing, singing, parades and fireworks to mark the occasion of a new ruler of Amun, but there would be no celebrating tonight. There was much to attend to with all of the injuries that surrounded us, and my mother's blood still covered the walls of our palace. It was late in the evening when I returned to my quarters. I was wet, dirty and freezing from the metal beadwork that adorned my body. My cherished little girl looked flushed in the face and sneezed over and over again while I tried to comfort her. Reo pushed me away and deliriously begged for the comfort and protection of her caregiver. It was the final insult to my day, and I broke down. I wanted my daughter, I wanted my mother, I wanted Leo, I wanted to be anywhere but here, anyone but me.

My heart broke as the rain fell relentlessly for the next two days. I spent those days shutting out the world around me and my precious daughter as I planned my revenge. I knew the Others would be back, but there was no telling when or where they would appear or what their plan could be. We knew so little about them it was impossible to properly organize our defense. With this in mind I spared no action and designed multiple possibilities to safeguard our people in the event of an attack from any direction. I did not rest for days, and then was ordered to rest by my grandmother who felt my anger was getting the best of me. We had begun to argue over small details. It was unfamiliar to both of us to feel such animosity towards each other. I felt I was seeing a side

of her I had never known. I longed for the grandmother of my youth, but knew that woman would
only exist for my daughter now. I begrudgingly returned to my quarters to rest my body and mind.
Somewhere in the middle of the night as I slept,
the rain stopped, I am not sure exactly when, but
it was shortly before I awoke in the dark hours of
morning. The moment my guards woke me I knew
something was wrong, I could feel it all around
me.

PART THREE

THE WAVE

THE WAVE

It was the darkest hour before dawn when they alerted me that the water was gone. At first, I believed my guards and grandmother were speaking of the water that had fallen relentlessly from our sky. "Queen Kala," my guards insisted, "the water at the beach has gone. The fishermen are unable to begin their day's work and your guidance is needed immediately." I could not understand how the ocean water was gone as it had been nothing but an endless downpour since the coronation. I knew I must leave the comforts of my bed and investigate immediately.

I feared this might be a ploy to lure me from the palace, and so I left my sleeping child with my grandmother as I departed for the beach with six of my guards. We travelled quickly through the darkness to the beach cove where the fisherman and their children had gathered. As sure as they claimed, the water at the beach was indeed missing, it had receded back as far as the eye could see. My first instinct was to look around for any sign of the Others and their iridescent spheres. I felt it too strong a coincidence that this should happen in their tense absence.

I looked around to familiarize myself with the environment to see if there was a logical reasoning for this before we should panic people. There were many people around me when I arrived, and as the minutes passed more were flocking to marvel at the oddity. For miles around the water had receded and left exposed slick white mud and thousands of colorful floundering fish. Strange looking rocks stuck out of the mud where the water would usually cover them. They reminded me of darkly corroded bones, like those we kept in the burial chambers of our ancestors.

The breeze suddenly picked up, and I searched the sky for answers. In the twilight I found an absence of life where there should be a feeding frenzy of birds picking off the muddy fish. The limestone cliffs behind me jutted up quite a distance to a flat grassy area above our heads, and so I sent a guard to scale the cliff and see if there was anything more that could be learned from a higher perspective. Nothing was making sense, and to make matters worse the fisherman stood around arguing, waiting for me to do something that would fix this inconvenience. I felt a terrible pressure from inside my head that made me feel like I was sinking into the ground.

Despite the stress of the adults gathered around, the children played cheerfully in the mud trying the catch the large fish that were flopping around. The smaller children formed mud bowls and patties to feed their mud shaped dolls while others laughed and slid around in the chalky clay muck. A small group of children began hauling the strange rocks sticking out from the muck and arranged them on the shoreline. The fisherman yelled back and forth about how they will make no catch today because all of the boats are stuck in the mud. The boats all lay on their sides and risked damage from the pressure. There was a mix of marvel and exasperation amongst the crowd, and it felt like they all turned at once to look to me for guidance.

The sun was coming up and you could see the golden light begin to glow from behind the furthest point of the waters receding. The illumination of the oceans absence was truly unsettling and it began to agitate the gathering. I led the people in a meditation on the beach, and tried to communicate with Oona and find answers. I was unsuccessful in communicating with her and instead saw the leaking wooden door from my youth. The water began to spurt out from around the cracks of the door at such a great pace that I felt water begin to gather at my feet. I strongly felt that I needed to leave this place. I opened my eyes and led the others to do the same. We were all standing in a small amount of water which had suddenly reappeared at our feet. The fisherman celebrated and thanked me for my efforts.

I was feeling incredibly lucky and suddenly exhausted. The water placidly started to surge in, like a gentle trickle that was suddenly all around us. A small wave crashed at my feet where there was rippled sand only moments before. I was relieved that there was an answer to the missing tide before I was required to do much more. I looked out at the rising sun, its golden pink aura bursting over the horizon. My body was tired and on edge. I felt the immensity of my new role and it was crushing.

My guards told me I was needed back at the palace for other duties, so I bid good luck to the fisherman on their day's catch and turned with my guards to leave the beach. On the pebbled shore in front of me stood a boy, no more than 10 years old. I saw the child point out to the water behind me and his face was a mask of pure terror. There was something behind me that had ripped the soul from his eyes. I felt electricity pulse through my body as I turned and looked in the direction of his accusing finger.

Out of the very corner of my eye I saw it, and instantly wished I had never turned to see such a monstrosity. Even in the thousands of years that have passed since I first laid eyes on it, I can still see the wave as clearly as on that fateful day. It is forever engraved in my mind and will remain a part of me for all my eternal existence. It stood many times taller than any mountain or cliff that stretched across our land. The waves' energy grew as it roared towards us with its white capped fangs poised to devour. It was so powerful you could feel the energy of it, ready to come crashing down and smother everything we have ever known to be home into a million pieces.

Everyone on the beach was standing around stunned by the reality of what stood before us. As the leader of Amun, I know I should have tried to help those around me get to higher ground, but there was such enormity to the wave I truly did not believe it possible for any of us to survive it. My body ran on pure adrenaline and instinct as I turned to the limestone cliffs that jutted up behind me into the skies. I began to climb as quickly as I could, trying every heartwrenching moment to get back to my daughter. I needed to hold Reo as this monstrosity enveloped our world, and if need be, depart it with her. I climbed swiftly and felt I could hardly breathe as I put one hand over the other, ripping the skin from my hands and feet as I tried to get to Reo. I knew the wave was getting closer from the screams I began to hear coming from all directions around me. The wave had come to destroy us and there was nowhere to hide.

I was nearly to the top and felt an electric surge within me to go faster. The sound of the wave was starting to hurt my ear drums, I knew it grew closer without having to look. Right as I was about to place my hand on the top ledge and pull myself onto the grassy bluff, I felt this strange energy envelope my body and absorb me. At first I thought it was the wave, and I am too late, but instead found myself trapped within a strange capsule. I realized with a sickening jolt that it was one of the spheres the Others had travelled to Amun in. The same exact spheres I saw that eventful evening when they first appeared in the sky off my balcony. I could not remove myself from the sphere, nor break my way through it.

The sphere lifted me rapidly to a height above the wave. The pull of the mechanism made my insides feel like they had been pulled down from my body. As great an effort as I could make, I banged on the sides, kicked, scratched and screamed. Not a dent was made, and I was helpless to watch the water rushing in at all angles below me, dragging the bodies of the fisherman, their children and all the onlookers into the sea. The sphere then pulled my body into a suspended state and forced my eyelids open to watch the rest unfold.

The wave was so near, I shook as I watched it tower above the palace. My eyes transfixed on the palace, I could identify my private balcony from this height. I knew my daughter slept innocently in my bed just a stone's throw from that platform which was quickly becoming inundated with murky surges. I begin to vomit at the thought of my child being submerged into the murky, debris filled water. I feel the cold sense of total annihilation and I cannot look away. The water moved with such ferocity, the wave was alive and ready to eat. It crashed with a deafening roar on top of Lymuria. I felt my daughter's life force rip away from me quickly, and then a moment later, my grandmothers. I could not move, I could not think. I could only stare at the chaos that unfolded as the sphere transported me at the wave's pace and forced me to watch my kingdom fall into a watery grave.

The Liquid mountain collapsed onto my city and dispersed with such force that it exploded everything in its path. The water rushed through the streets and the houses, taking with it everything without a shred of descrimination for size or stature. The flower covered roads submerged under charcoal colored surges of water, while masses of birds and insects fled the limbs only to be absorbed into the waves path. Wooden houses floated down the streets, their inhabitants clung to each other unsteadily as they lay on the roofs of these unsteerable vessels.

Many disappeared under the dark gray water as the houses broke apart and burst their contents into the air. I watched the glass dome with the tree of life pattern that had covered me only days before at my coronation, shatter onto those underneath it. The large shards of glass joined the debris within the surge that sliced the thousands who were pulled in its current. The streets turned to river rapids, pulling all those shopping and selling on its well stocked market streets into the deluge. Droves of people ran from it, but none could out run it, as there was no final place of safety to flee to. Clusters of people trampled each other as they rushed towards a higher ground that would never be high enough.

Boats turned upside down crashed into the stone buildings our ancestors had built, splintering the structures and impaling people with wooden shards in its wake. Desperate women took their babies and held them up in the air as if someone would grab them, but there was no one above to save them. Mother and child together were sucked into the angry dark swell. Children were pulled from the arms of their fathers who ran like beheaded chickens seeking a shelter that would only be found in death. Many tried to swim or float but they too were quickly sucked under the raging flow.

The screaming, you could hear the screaming everywhere. My people could do nothing in the face of such power except scream. Nature's roar competed with the people for their death lament. It was a chorus of millions in anguish, it was a sound I hope I never hear again. I wanted to rip my eyes out, bash my head against the sphere and join my people.

Without warning, I saw that there was a second wave crashing in from an opposing direction. When the two waves met, it created a whirlpool that became a swirling collection of the ruins of our great civilization. The outer rim of the island of Amun was mostly made of volcanic rock and limestone that served previously as a natural defense system. Instead it now served as the rim of a bowl, keeping the massive amount of displaced water stuck within our homeland. Hundreds of thousands of bodies lay below me floating face-down in the muck.

The final deathblow was given when a third wave appeared from another direction that encircled the island and submerged it permanently below the water. Large vents of steam poured out from deep beneath the water, and a strange shaking occurred as the earth beneath the water cracked apart. I searched in my hysteria for anything that may remain, but there was nothing recognizable left. In just a few moments Amun too, was gone. The woven blanket of debris and dirty water was her burial shroud.

Scattered amongst the rising water were a few unlucky enough to survive. They clung to the tops of the jagged rock that dotted the new ocean spanse. The piles of debris began to shake loose in some areas and floated out to sea with many still alive unwillingly using these mounds as rafts. Hungry sea life circled them, waiting for their inevitable meal. Above them, the sky turned to ash and covered the survivors and made it difficult to see and breathe. On the horizon, I saw explosions erupting from all directions in the water, as more waves were born and began their journey to the carcass of Amun to ensure its eternal destruction.

Somewhere behind me, the sun tried to poke a ray out from behind the heavy ash that littered the air. It dawned on me all at once that it was all gone, that my baby was gone. I would never hold her head against my body again. I felt something inside me snap, and I screamed until I felt blood trickle down my throat.

This was the prophecy. We had just been too blind to see it.

PART FOUR

ATLANTIS

ATLANTIS

There was no way to know how long I stayed in the blacked out world of in-between during my journey in the sphere. Upon arrival to the island of Atlantis, Osiris had me jolted awake from my stupor with an injection to my upper arm that caused my heart to race and my eyes to bulge from their sockets. At first I could not focus on what I saw before me, my vision was blurred and the cobblestoned streets they stealthily led me through were poorly lit. I could not turn my head or move my limbs due to the constraints the Others tied around my body. I felt like a criminal. My clothes were torn and covered in vomit and blood, much of which also embedded itself into my hair. I could smell the stench of death all around me. An acrid scent of burning hair scorched my nostrils. The Others all wore tight fitting black masks similar to the ones I had first seen upon their arrival to Amun. I saw no other signs of life around me despite the many buildings and homes that we passed in the night. I felt something bad had happened here. Something frantic, something unpleasant. You could see signs of it all around.

I was led through the gaping mouth of a large tunnel that went underneath a wide canal. We travelled quickly through the rounded passageway and emerged out of the tunnel into the night world of their capital city, Poseida. A massive fountain greeted us in a large cobblestone square that was flanked by magnificent buildings with ornately carved facades. The fountain depicted the beginnings of Poseida, and showed a half submerged spaceship crashed into the water. In front of it emerged their founder Atlas, triumphantly holding a replica of their Red Crystal. There was a mist sprayed by masked individuals around the square, they followed behind us to ensure we brought in nothing that would sicken the people. The mist irritated my eyes and skin. Itchy red welts began to rise up on my limbs and torso, but there was no way to find relief while I was tied up like an animal.

I could tell the Others have an island that was very sophisticated and advanced. It was nothing like Amun in its architectural style or feel. The cylindrical structures that flanked the streets launched high into the air, creating a narrow canyon of buildings that blocked out nearly all of the moonlight. There was a very negative energy that emanated from the streets of this island, I could feel how it creates a deep rooted anxiety and competitive nature amongst its inhabitants. There was a coldness in the air that night, a feeling my skin was not familiar with. It was a stinging fridgidness that my tropical homeland never allowed me to experience before. One of my captors took his baton and cracked the back of my leg for not moving fast enough. The pain reverberated through to the very tips of my frozen toes as I struggled to continue putting one foot in front of the other. My ankle rolled when the uneven cobblestones caught my step once again. Another of my masked captors grabbed me by my hair and pulled me down the street at pace with the grouping of the Others. Finally, he let go when a clump of my hair was pulled out.

I was forced to stand and continued to limp alongside my captors as blood trickled from my scalp. Eventually, I was brought to the front of a building that had no windows and no signage. The building was long and grey, its blank exterior gave no clues to its purpose. Suddenly, bright white light poured onto our small crowd as two masked men appeared at the large metal door that had split open before us. My eyes burned from the light and I closed them shut tightly. I was unable to do anything as they shackled me to a longboard and transported me into the facility. That was the last I would see of the outside world for the next two years.

In the confines of this facility, I slowly began to piece together the hidden world around me. What I gathered was that the virus had devastated Atlantis for nearly three years before my arrival and nearly caused a collapse of their society. When Osiris came to Amun he was on the verge of being overthrown, he had lost the belief of the masses that once gathered around him. I could feel that there had been a heavy loss of life here that had occurred quite suddenly. I know many died, because I would smell the scent of burning each day. I believe they burned the dead and put their ashes into mass graves sealed with a tar like substance. I could never forget the smell, it was the same smell of the pungent hot ooze we used in Amun to waterproof structures. It made my head ache behind my eyes, and caused me to become so nauseous that I would dry heave for hours with the vile scent stuck to the back of my throat.

My captors at this time were the many guards and scientists who passed me off to each other throughout the day. They all embodied the same methodical Atlantean coldness that was rude and abrupt at its best. I watched them float around me as they jabbed and prodded, absorbed into their private little worlds, glimpsing outwards only to judge another within its orbit. Equally aware of my pain and suffering, they made no effort to treat me humanely. I was experimented on without consideration or mercy. My only act of defense was that I showed them nothing of my inner self, I closed myself off and spoke no words. Still, they persisted in finding within me something they were not entirely sure of. The first test they performed had me placed into a large glass tube that scanned my body and gave them detailed information about my genetic history.

Sometimes, Osiris would appear in my cell late at night. We would stare each other down in the darkness of the windowless cell for ages before he would finally begin to rage and unleash his frustrations on me. He would throw his arms around and insult me and my people. Osiris screamed all kinds of threats and called for my death, but we both knew I was his only link to the answer he needed to save himself. When he finished with his tirade he would leave and make a point to slam the heavy metal door behind him. As always, he would then have my food cut off for the next two days and would return on the third day and taunt me with food in the face of my starvation. I could see how his people would be scared of him, and over time I could see in my captors' eyes that they were beginning to question Osiris' brute authority. I often wondered if I would outlast his reign, if any of us would survive Osiris.

I was painfully aware that I was constantly under surveillance in the facility. They used a device to watch me in my cell, and its ominous gaze steadily followed me through the day to the many laboratories I was forced into. The constant monitoring was meant to dehumanize me and likewise, prevent me from killing myself. Had I the means, I would have parted from this earthly body early on in my Atlantean imprisonment. Life inside the facility was a true challenge for anyone wanting to end their sentence early. There was no bed or furniture in the cell, nor loose objects, just a heavy door with a food slot on the bottom that locked shut. My body ached constantly from the cold floor I slept on.

The scientists shaved my head and body for years to aid in their experimentations. One early test was particularly brutal. A male scientist placed a metal probe into my backside which ripped from the pressure. The fissures inside went on for years and years, well into my old age. The constant cycle of torturous experiments and sitting on a cold floor took its toll and kept the wound cyclically open, often bleeding and swelling. The pain was unbearable, and even the idea of my next meal brought on a nervous frenzy of paranoia. I could not be sure, but I felt that they were putting something in my food to worsen the condition. After I would eat a few bites of the lukewarm porridge made of yellow grain and rendered animal fat, my stomach would gurgle and cramp. Starving myself into a slow death had been an early plan, but it never lasted long when the feeding tube was a much easier method of forcefully delivering my nutrients. At least when I did the feeding, I could control exactly how much I ate, as opposed to the massive amounts they literally shoved down my throat.

I remember it was always so brutal and shockingly cold in their laboratories. I was treated as nothing more than an animal to be experimented on, and looked at with no more value. Since they could not understand what they were looking for, it was inevitable they would not be successful in their search of me. During the endless hours of my experimentation, I would study my captors and could tell many of them did not want to be there, but instead of compassion they showed me indifference. There were quite a few that did want to be there, some that truly found a hidden pleasure in hurting me. If I did not keep up with their quick pace or commands they dragged me with my arms tied behind my back and returned me roughly to my cell with a forceful toss. I was pushed down onto floors and pushed up against walls, even suspended by my ankles from the ceiling.

I could see the broken coldness in their eyes; they did not care if I survived my experiments. My skin erupted into a blanket of itchy red welts that were pushed to the surface by my terror and anxiety. The skin at my knuckles began to break apart from the swelling and crusted over with infection. They were so dry and itched so badly, as were my knees and elbows, but I could not remove the itch no matter how hard I scratched. I soon had bloody patches on all my joints and eventually itchy scabs that took years to harden into overgrown calluses. I begged my captors for relief from the incessant itching, I was met with dead eyes and blank stares, as if I had not spoken at all.

My defiance was the only thing I could control, and so I used it often. When the guards were instructed to beat me for my disobedience, I used a technique my grandmother showed me when I trained in the Moves of War. The technique was meant to bring a soul to peace before it died in battle, so as not to bring the trauma forward with it to the next life. The guards kicked my head and my torso in my cell, and while I performed the technique, I felt less pain, I felt removed, I felt peace. Later, I felt the pain, but I am alone and can nurse myself away from scrutinizing eyes. When I tried late at night to communicate with my family, I heard only the voice of my mother's spirit telling me to stay alive. She whispered to me that the energy cannot die with me, I must stay alive long enough to pass it on. My anger boiled over and I wanted to lash out and rage, but I am in too much pain to move. I wanted to die, I wanted to be with my child. I wanted her back in my arms. Instead, I am to remain alive in Atlantis, indefinitely.

It was inevitable that I would one day become exposed to their virus. The immunity powers of Amun were long destroyed with the island and I had been in poor health during my captivity. I knew it was near when I saw many of my captors disappear suddenly and replaced by others after a sudden burst of vomiting. When the virus found its way to me, it arrived suddenly and without warning or expectation. What I would have welcomed only weeks before had now become something I must fight against and win.

My head began to spin and the walls swirled around me as I expelled liquid from every orifice of my body. The small white cell I was held in began to fill with waste and the stench only added to my cycle of heaving. My muscles felt like they were being ripped off my body. I was sore and unable to move, my body burned with delirious fever. I cried out for help, but my body was so dry I could not form words at my cracked lips. I was ready to give up my life to this virus. I closed my eyes tight as I spasmed through a dry heave and blacked out.

Suddenly, I saw my grandmother before me. She held her hand out as if to push me away. She looked angry with me. I realized with overwhelming vexation that she was sending me back. I screamed for her embrace, but she was firm in her position. I woke on the cold floor of the cell and around me were two guards in full protective gear lifting me onto a transport gurney. They stuck a needle in my arm and passed fluid into my body, I could feel its coldness travel through my veins and start to fill my body back up. The scientists in the facility could not understand why I was still alive. There had been no such recovery from the virus before this, and my experiments continued in full force with this novel discovery.

My captors began using a new device to look

inside my body after my recovery from the virus. There was a large tube they would bring me to. They would lay me down and slowly push my body into the small opening of the tube. Once inside, there was barely room to breathe, let alone move any limbs. The more you squirmed or sighed, the longer the machine would take to gain its results, so it was imperative I stay still and get the procedure over with. There would be a sudden jolt of sound that would pierce your ears when they began their work, it would alternate with other sounds that would hit points in my ear drum that felt at times like they would bore small holes in them.

The shattering sounds would eventually cause visions to appear before the darkness of my closed eyes. I would see terrifying things, mounds of mud with hands sticking out, reaching for my body, pulling me into their private hell. These sessions would go on for hours and hours. I felt my sanity begin to waver from these repetitive tortures. I studied my captors to stay sane. I hoped for any abnormality in their routine that I might take advantage of and attempt some disruption to my derangement.

One day, a rare moment presented itself. A new scientist had forgotten to lock me up properly before an experiment began. When she excused herself to consult the male doctor for authority to begin, I was able to slip away and move quickly down the hallway to the staircase. I could feel the cameras following me, I knew it would not be long before the guards caught up. It probably brought more attention to me that I was running. Had I taken a moment and maybe used some material to disguise myself I probably would have gotten further, but it was so quick an instinct that there was no plan. I ran from everyone and no one in particular. I saw a door open ahead of me as a group of scientists were entering the facility for their shift. I gained all the momentum I could and barreled into them, knocking them to the ground. They seemed more scared of me than willing to stop me, and so I sprinted for the door. I felt the air on my skin for the first time in years, but I knew I could not stop to enjoy it.

During the two years of my imprisonment I had become as weak as an elderly woman. My muscles had atrophied, and my swollen, scabby joints made for difficult passage. Even so, I persisted and scurried towards a bridge in the distance. I remembered this bridge from when I first came to Atlantis, it was above the tunnel we took to enter into the innermost ring of the capital. I know this bridge will lead me out of this moated hell. I limped up the ramp and struggled to continue on foot.

I was not yet at the halfway mark across the bridge when I saw the guards coming towards me from the other side. Running alongside them were black jungle cats, sharp toothed killer beasts that have been trained to turn me into a meal. My heart struggled to pump as I gasped for breath and looked for another escape route. A quick glance around proved to me my options were slim as I watched guards closing in on me from each side of the bridge. Seeing no other choice, I pulled myself up onto the cold grey metal pole that acted as a guard rail, and jumped from the bridge to my best option.

It was a long way down to the water. I fell for what felt like a small eternity, and watched the world that had been hidden away from me spread out in all its glory. The water underneath me was part of a wide circular mote that encircled Poseida. In the short distance, I could see two other circular motes further surrounding the city. As I fell, there was something that caught my attention on the water's edge, it was a peculiar attraction for the upper class Atlanteans who would ride carts on tracks into the water. The carts would submerge them into the depths of the crystal clear moat where they would be able to breathe underwater.

As I hit the water, I was stunned but unhurt. I sank down in the heavy depths, but was surprised to find I had no trouble breathing underwater. The Atlanteans had done something to the water I could not explain, it allowed you to breathe as effortlessly as one would on land. The water was easy to glide in, and I moved swiftly despite the initial shock of cold. As I swam underwater, I passed by a family of four who were bewildered to encounter me during their underwater ride. The mother and father both were alarmed by my presence and reached for their children as I crossed their underwater path. They covered their children's eyes as if I was too offensive to look at.

As I persisted to find a way out of Atlantis, my body began to cramp from the decline of my muscles. I swam towards the shoreline and found an easy spot to pull myself up from alongside a wall of boulders propped against the base of the bridge. The roughness of the rocks cut my hands, and left a bloody path of handprints as I forced my body over the stone wall that sat on top of the boulders. I hoisted my body over the wall and fell to the ground as I rolled my ankle during my rough landing. Around me there was a terrace where the bridge connected to the land of the innermost circle of Poseida. As I took in my surroundings to reconfigure my escape, I realized I was in the midst of a very elite looking waterside restaurant where very affluent people have come to celebrate. Dotted amongst the crowd were numerous waiters carrying large trays of seafood and large bottles of liquor with many sparkling glasses. I was painfully aware that I was making a scene. Everyone around was frozen and looked at me with disdain and annoyance. I was surprised to see none of these people wore a mask. Since my first day in Atlantis I had not seen the complete face of any of their citizens. They all looked very similar to me, with their silvery white hair and vivid eyes.

There was a scuffle amongst the crowd when I made the first move to exit. Many jumped from their chairs to scatter away from me. One did not stray, though- a young boy of 5 or 6 remained in front of me, unshaken. His ocean blue eyes pierced into my soul and locked my gaze. It was only for a moment, but it felt like he stole a shred of me. In that moment, the young boy and I, we can see each other from the other's perspective. I see who I have become, I am desperate, and un-recognizable to the woman I once knew. My grey streak has grown wider while my skin has turned a sallow yellow, and wrinkled around my many sores and scabs. I choked down my grief as I real-ized the woman I was has died. Something in the boy's sharp eyes warmed, and suddenly, he smiled at me as time seemed to freeze around us.

Behind me, a crash of glass to the ground turned my attention and I panicked when I saw the guards and their vicious cats have found me once again. These were no ordinary cats the guards controlled from long leather harnesses. These were the same as the vicious cats that par-aded wildly around the jungles of our colonies, but bred compactly to make an aggressive kill-ing machine. As the cats encircled me, the iri-descent travel spheres of Osiris appeared. The crowd dispersed and Osiris approached me alone. He taunted me and my pitiful escape attempt. "Where will you go?" He questioned with a wry smile on his face. And then I realized that he had a valid point, I do not know where I will run to. It is all gone. They are all dead. "You watched them die, who will you return to? He taunted as if pulling it from my mind as each thought appeared.

And in that moment of self-doubt and insecurity, I hesitated. I should have done anything but stopped, but stop I did. And with that, they grabbed me and threw me to the ground and kicked me in my head until I saw black. My last thought before the darkness was that I had lost my only chance. The Atlanteans would never be that careless again in my treatment, and now I would spend the rest of my life in this horrible place. However long they would let that be. I now know I will never leave Atlantis alive. Jumping off the bridge was the furthest that I would ever get to freedom.

When I awoke from my beating, I was back in the facility and strapped to an icy metal table where they introduced me to a new type of scientific torture. The scientists flashed a violet colored light over and over again in a small dark room as my eyes felt like they would bulge from my head. The flashing caused me to hallucinate large shadowy creatures emerging in the darkness that were getting closer to me with each outburst of light. I wanted to close my eyes and project my mind elsewhere, but I was wary that they would see into me during these experiments and learn too much of my powers. I could feel myself slip in and out of madness with each flash of the violet light. For the first few years they performed many experiments like this on me. Over time, the experiments changed in nature and eventually descended into all out torture sessions.

One of the worst things they would do involved innocent people from Atlantis, a collection of slaves, laborers, rogue politicians and even their children. They would put me amongst the seized Atlanteans in a large hole in the ground that had smooth, stone walls. The hole was deep and once inside, you could not climb out. The people would nervously gather around and then one by one, they would see me and begin to react nervously to my presence. As more would notice me the masses would move as far away as possible, thinking I was the threat they had been set against.

Each time it was the same, and each time a massive drop of water covered these people and filled the gorge as I was lifted above them in a sphere. Over and over again, they would force me to watch as they drowned their own people. I would have to watch as their bodies floated to the top and were skimmed off the water like insects. Afterwards, they would play the sounds of those people screaming and dying all through the night so I could not sleep. Their shrieks would ring through my ears and bring back the horror of the wave that destroyed my homeland.

Their use of water in my torture did not

end there. I was often brought to a room that held a long, narrow water tank and submerged relentlessly. I believed they wanted to see if my powers would kick in during my panicked response to the drowning simulation. My tormentors would sometimes bring me to the brink of blackness and then release me, other times they let me go without breath for several minutes before I chose to come back. I always chose to come back, not because I wanted to punish myself, but I knew I could not let what was inside of me die and end with me. I somehow would have to go on, and even though I could not see how that would unfold, I had to trust it would.

There were days when it was very hard to believe that staying alive was the right choice. I fell into a deep depression, and my obvious lethargy only resulted in me being sent to the lab for shock therapy. The technicians would place numerous electric rods on my skull and also on my lower spine. The pain would reverberate throughout my body without mercy, blinding my sight with bright white light. The current grew so powerful during a session one day that I bit off the very tip of my tongue. From then on my speech was never the same. Words became difficult to form and I soon gave up talking all together. Over time, I forgot the sound of my voice.

After the shock therapy failed they began to isolate me for long periods of time. For months on end I was submerged in darkness and my experiments became few and far between. I noticed a change in the guards and staff in the facility. The familiar faces I had associated with my many torments were slowly replaced, and over time, I noticed all the women who had once worked there disappeared. The new guards that I did come into contact with were not as interested in abusing me, they seemed preoccupied with their own survival, worried about something beyond my windowless prison.

In the darkness of my narrow cell I would try and meditate but was often afraid they were monitoring me, so I never stayed too long or went too deep into trance. I was able to go to a place in my mind where I could silently hide and let time pass quickly. It was something very unique to having my senses dulled and being deprived of light, fresh air, and human touch. This little pocket of the mind allowed me to speed up time in small ways, but it would mostly help shorten the duration of my chronic pain.

Every so often, these beings of energy from the home planet would intercept my meditation. I could feel what they were trying to say, they were telling me to be patient. Many years passed and I continued to see less and less of my guards until one day, my food was not delivered. Usually, if Osiris was to punish me with hunger it went on for no more than three days, but this time, it was different. It felt as if they had forgotten about me, and my abandonment was less a form of deliberate punishment. For days I sat and waited for any signs of life around me. My mouth turned to sand and my stomach moaned from emptiness.

I had no visits from Osiris, nor heard any footsteps or conversations of guards. I had not taken part in an experiment for years, but often would hear the voices of the scientists at the facility. Now, I heard nothing but the hum of the mechanism that created the air I breathed. I wondered if they had found the key to my powers and now I had been left to die slowly within these four blank walls. The possibility of death worried and overjoyed me at the same time. I wondered what I would say to my mother when my energy crossed over? I know I have failed to pass the energy on, but I cannot see how it will ever be possible to do such a transfer when I consider the world around me.

Before I die, I prepare myself by going within my mind and bring peace to my tormented body while withdrawing from the monotony around me. I felt a jolt in my body, like a snap in electricity and I knew I was close to the end. I focused and breathed deeply and began to feel the upward pull of myself away from my body. Into the light I floated, so happy to be relieved of this mess of an existence. I saw a face before me, it was my spirit guide Oona. I was delighted to be with her again, but she was upset at the sight of me.

Oona told me I have been forgotten on Earth, but my celestial home will never forget me.

I am free to communicate with them as I like, but I am not to leave my earthly body. "They have found an answer without you and created an entirely new type of energy," she informed. "This is what they were destined to do, and now have no need for your powers. You will be able to use them as you see fit until the time comes for you to join us. You will know when the time will come, there will be many signs." I challenged Oona and demanded to know how I am to survive on Earth. I reminded her that with no food or water my body will not function. "Trust that it is unfolding as it should be," she replied to my despair.

I could feel the pull of the Earth bringing me back, magnetizing me to its core. A sudden jolt and I found myself back in my cell. My face was wet, and a steady drip of water fell into my mouth from the circular light fixture above me. Somewhere in the facility a pipe had burst, and its rush of water had begun to revive my dehydrated body. It was not long before a team sent to repair the leak came across my nearly dead body and brought it to the attention of the staff at the facility. I remember them moving me on a cart to another wing of the building, and when I awoke, I had a tube down my throat that was force feeding me.

They asked me who I was, as they were all new staff and said they did not have records on me. I could not and would not answer them. It was safer if no one knew who I was. I was placed in a new cell by my new captors. My accommodations were similar to the one I had left behind, but now I was closer to other prisoners and could hear the far off mutterings of the incarcerated. My meals appeared again, and I continued my cycle of survival until the day was to come when I would be allowed to leave this miserable existence.

Years passed as I sat in that cell. During the endless hours I would sometimes try to contact Oona and the ancient ones, and ask them what was the fate of my people and my child. I had tried several years ago to communicate with the soul of my daughter Reo. I found her once, but she was stuck in a place where she was always frightened and would not come to my light. Reo does not understand what happened to her or what happened to me and remains lost in the in-between place. I feel she has millions of companions in this dark place from the motherland, all lost in the deluge and stuck in a swirling eddy of anguish. I took no comfort in knowing that she was not alone there.

Oona transfers to me the vision of masses of my people gathered in unknown places of the netherworld, stuck and confused, still not aware that they are dead. I have been afraid that they are still able to monitor me at the facility, so I am very careful about how far I go into trance and what I ask of my spirit guide. My inquiries are concise and direct, I need to know if I will ever leave this place, and if my child was truly gone. It hurts for Oona to tell me because she has been communicating with me my entire life, and the truth was very overbearing.

Instead, she showed me how my daughter was ripped from the arms of my grandmother by the force of the wave and her beautiful little skull impaled on an iron hook that hung from a palace wall. My grandmother was launched headfirst into one of the intricately cut walls of the palace. She was knocked unconscious from the waves force and her lungs swiftly filled with water as her body took its last breath. Oona assured me they died very quickly and I am thankful for that. Oona shared with me the fate of many who survived the initial wave, only to be subjected to agonizingly slow deaths.

Many were left clinging to the very tops of the mountains and remained submerged in ash and darkness while Amun sunk beneath them. The last people of my island clung together, reasonless and numb at first. They were ultimately forced to survive by means of cannibalism on the small island tops left in the great ocean spanse. I saw them cry and gag as they were forced to eat the flesh of those who offered themselves up for the survival of others. They lived in filth and darkness until their numbers dwindled down to just a few. Eventually they descended from the rocks that stuck out of the water as the sea returned to its aqua color. They learned to push long bamboo poles into the sand and began to build huts on the top of them. To these survivors, the memory of my family became a curse, a legend of catastrophic womanly rule to put fear into future generations.

There were some who escaped by floating on debris rafts to some of our colonies that were not as hard hit by the wave. One group of people in particular were situated to the west of our Empire where a large volcano provided shelter for several thousand who outran the watery onslaught. These people made their way to a large colony across the water, to a group of people my mother had been working with right before her death and the arrival of the Others. The colonists told tales of a tremendous ancient structure to the west of Amun shaped like the square jawed jungle cat that hunted the lands around them. The cat structure had sparked an interest in my mother, she needed to know more about the statue and why the ancients would have built such a structure. Our legends told of powerful technology brought from the home planet that was stored beneath the left paw of such a statue.

Oona told me that Leo had been sent on the journey to the monument by my mother to see what connection it might have to the Others. Along with three other men from the colony, they journeyed together for months along a red soil path in search of the feline monolith. Their conditions were not ideal, they sweltered in the humid summer heat while constantly being hunted by the hungry jungle cats. Leo and the colonists were unlucky in their hunt and went many days without eating. Frustrated and tired, Leo and his companions began to argue when hunger got the best of them.

When they arrived at the vine covered statue of the jungle cat they were astonished by its size and magnificence. The jungle cat's head stood seven stories above them and its body stretched out majestically for quite a distance. There was a strange pull they all had to this mystery in stone. Leo and the three colonists camped underneath the statue and all dreamed of impending doom. It was a warning transferred from the eternal energy stored within the ancient stone beast. The group was so upset by the dreams that they turned around that same day and began their trek home to the colony. The journeymen bonded deeply over this shared vision and when they returned, they were greeted with the somber news of Amun's destruction.

Oona showed me Leo's face when he was told we are gone; that his child and I have been swept away in the wave. He rips at his face and screams for us. The colonists had to hold Leo down and tranquilize him to keep from scaring the children of the colony with his wailing.

Many refugees from Amun gathered in the colony and the once plentiful resources of the area could no longer sustain its population. Leo offered to lead a group of survivors and colonists to the jungle cat statue and begin a new colony there. There were many journeys back and forth, and endless trials and tribulations on the well worn red clay path. Leo heard the stories of those who survived during these travels and felt their power.

Over time, Leo found solace in helping the survivors of the wave restart their lives. Before Leo died, he created a beautiful book, bound in the finest of gold and parchment. Embossed in gold on the cover of his book, was a fully bloomed lotus flower, and beneath it, a snake. Leo's book was an ode to the people of Amun lost in the cataclysm, and his final way of finding peace with the loss of the family that I should have never denied him. He wrote our stories down, and the stories of the countless others to make sure the tales of our land carried on through the void of history, He called his tribute, "The Book of the Dead," and left it in the care of the colonists he had gathered in this new land.

What Leo did not know was that my mother's instinct on the jungle cat statue being connected to the Others was right. Had Leo passed the statue and continued his journey by boat, he would have encountered the island of Atlantis. This was the closest I ever was to being near any of my people again during my imprisonment on that dreadful island. Leo and I were the worst kind of soul mates, the kind that can never be. I should have left with him and Reo the night he asked me to, and I am given many years to torment myself with this self damning information. After receiving this information, it was many years before I decided to talk to my celestial ancestor again. My body was deteriorating rapidly from age and I felt my end approaching. I could not help but ask Oona what would become of my powers once I have passed them on. She would not give me an answer, but she does give me something.

It was an image she loaded into my mind of an infant many thousands of years from now. She has been smuggled out of a place that was destroyed and was hidden away in another part of the world to protect the power. Though it has weakened over the years, there was still divine awareness in this child even though she was not yet comprehending what she perceived. Oona will show me no more, she tells me I am to have patience, for I am near the end of my journey. I cannot find the faith within myself to believe her any longer. I felt it had all been in vain, that my sixty years in Atlantis will end as hopelessly as they began.

As I waited impatiently for death, I noticed there was a sudden increase in prisoners around me. I understood from what the other prisoners whispered in the night that a revolution was awakening Atlantis, and many facets looked to overthrow the tyrannical regime of Osiris. I began to hear the familiar sounds of torture, especially the electrical shocks they administered during their interrogations. The guards were merciless with the newcomers, many of whom I believed were there for making public their opposing views to Osiris and his regime. I tried to quiet my mind from the sounds of screaming and went within to connect with the ancient ones, but instead I was shown a flash of the young boy I encountered during my brief escape attempt many years ago. His crystal blue eyes were hypnotizing and held my gaze. He held his hand out to me, as if to join hands. I reached out and offered my hand out to the boy, but as our hands got closer I was jolted awake by the agonizing sounds of screaming from an adjoining cell. There was a sharp pain coming from my ear and a strange liquid slowly dripping from it. Over the next few days the pain in my ear increased and the pressure mounted. The infection had begun to distort my reality, and with the aid of the torture that abounded, I drifted in and out of consciousness, reliving my agonizing years of Atlantean experimentation in a cyclical hallucination. I felt paranoid, as if I was next at any moment, and they were coming to begin our experiments once more.

Though it sounded muffled from my ear infection, I heard someone slide food through the metal slot underneath my door and slam it shut. In my delirium, I did not notice that this time they did not come back for my bowl, nor any of the other prisoners. For three days we starved. I rolled myself into a ball on the floor as I cradled my throbbing ear and once again waited for death's belated approach. Instead of death, I heard muffled, distorted yelling down the corridors and around my cell. It confused me in my agitated state and full paranoia set in.

Suddenly, my door burst open, and several men entered and began questioning me with a chaotic fervor that combined to make a roar of nonsense. I could not understand them, and said nothing as I continued to lay there on the floor gripping my head, waiting for this all to end. Two more men joined them in the cell and helped to move me onto a wooden board and carried me out of the room. I did not feel myself as they wheeled me out of there. It felt like a part of my body could not leave that room, and would remain trapped there forever.

I remember the light outside was very intense and blinding when they carried me from the facility. I had not seen sunlight in many years, and my eyes burned as these men hurriedly transported me to a different medical facility. When I arrived, the doctors asked me who I was and what I was doing in Atlantis. My silence was my only response. I was placed on a cold metallic table that instantly reminded me of the laboratories in the facility and my many experiments.

Even though it had been many years since I had last been in that position, I was terrified they would begin again. I felt a disconnect going on between myself and these people. The exam the doctors tried to perform in the cold hospital room launched me into a panic. It was too much like the experiments and I coiled away at their touch. One worker moved to take blood from my arm with a long needle. I bit his arm and felt the other workers lunge for me immediately. I threw things around me and attacked them with whatever I could handle.

I needed to put space between myself and them and without realizing, backed myself into a corner. The guards entered the room and stormed towards me as I cowered in the corner. I felt degraded as I was held face down on the cold floor and crushed by four men until I felt my ribs break. I was thrown into a holding cell within the hospital, another windowless room, but ultimately, my final windowless room. My arms were tied to the bed in the holding cell as I painfully struggled to breathe and wished for this life to be over once and for all.

The hospital staff quickly became frustrated with me. I was a mystery to them as there was no paperwork on me to be found. Just as Oona had told me, I had been forgotten about. There had been so many changes of staff over the years no one could recall anything about me except that I needed to be fed. The doctors appealed to me and told me it was ok to talk, that I am now safe and Osiris was dead. I wish I could say it was a brutal death he suffered, equal to that of all the misery and torture he brought to my people, but perhaps that will be saved for another lifetime of his.

The doctors explained that early one morning, not so long ago, Osiris had a heart attack and laid in his waste all day waiting for help. He was not found until later that evening when his servants noticed that the trays of food brought to his door were still untouched. His servants were too afraid to disturb him during those hours, as the punishment was severe for any who disrupted his dealings. I can only hope Osiris suffered in those hours he lay covered in his waste, dying on the cold floor.

I would not be so lucky as to arrive at death's door as quickly as my old tormentor. For days on end I sat tied to a hospital bed, in and out of delirium, fighting against the technology they were using to revive my apathetic body. I was often given an injection that made my body go to sleep, but still was aware of many things around me. Sometimes, they would give me too much of this and I would see nothing but black.

The last injection I received was a heavy dose, possibly meant by a sympathetic doctor to ease my suffering. I danced in and out of worlds for many days, but I was greeted each time by my grandmother, who firmly held her hand out as if to say I may not enter. I cried for her to embrace me, but she would not approach, and remained steadfast in her obstruction.

When I finally opened my heavy eyes, I saw I was not alone in my hospital room. He stood before me at the foot of my bed, watching me sternly with his crystal blue eyes. Despite the years that had gone by, I knew immediately who he was, and I felt that he too recognized me even though we were now both elderly. Just like our first meeting so long ago during my escape attempt, our eyes locked and I felt our minds switch once more. I could see myself from his perspective, and I could see why he had come for me at last.

PART FIVE

THE JUDGE

THE JUDGE

My window faced out into a small courtyard that held many floors below, a decorative pond with metallic fish of many colors. The window stretched from the floor to the ceiling as one single pane. I could stand before it and feel my toes tingle as my body responded to the dizzying drop so close to me. I would stand for hours before this window and stare out into the small courtyard. I would try not to think about how my daughter would have loved to watch the shining colors float lazily in their water refuge. Luckily, I was not alone in my new window filled world. The blue eyed child from my escape attempt nearly six decades prior was now an aging Judge, one of the highest in all of Atlantis. The Judge had seen to it that I was promptly released from the hospital and given comfortable living quarters in a tall cylindrical building very close to his own home in the Atlantean capital, Poseida.

Where I lived, there was much metal and concrete in the building's sleek modern construction, and many technological marvels that were found within. In my living quarters there were cubed devices that cooked food very quickly, and systems to make the room temperature to your exact liking. I was surprised to see the Atlanteans had a system that spread information into the homes of people living in the capital. I was amazed at how they were able to spread the messages through our buildings in an instant, but I was also very aware of how these devices were meant to watch us as well. It was on this device that the Judge saw footage of me strapped to the hospital bed after my liberation by the new government of Atlantis. I know I should despise the spying box on the wall, but it has played a delicate role in my survival.

The Judge immediately took control of my case and tried to free me, but with no paperwork to comment on why I was imprisoned, the new government was hesitant to release me. My attack on the hospital staff did not help to show me as a non-violent threat to their society, and so I was ordered to stay within the confines of my quarters unless I was with the Judge. The Atlantean government offered that after a period of good behavior they would consider letting me go home. During my interactions with the new government, I was surprised and insulted to find there was no societal understanding of what had been done to my homeland so long ago by Osiris. Even in the dawn of their revolution, the Atlanteans were still ignorant and disillusioned with their nation's calamitous role in history.

As for the Judge, I could feel he was different from the other Atlanteans. I believed it was somehow linked to the otherworldly exchange that we had early on in his life. That exchange is what drove him to find me, he needed to know more about what that experience was. He said he was able to connect and suddenly understand his ancient origins during our unexpected meeting. It created a difference in him, a shift he said, but I saw that he buried this part of him deep within in order to blend in amongst his people. I could see the other Atlanteans believed the Judge was part of this mindset, but I knew this was a trait he learned in order to survive the dictatorship of Osiris.

I spent quite a bit of time walking with the Judge at night while the rest of Poseida slept. We would walk the inner circle of the city, on a wooden boardwalk that went around the perimeter of a canal that encircled Poseida. The water was always beautifully lit up by an underwater lighting system that gave the water a prismatic appearance. At first, there was not much to say between the two of us, but the Judge broke the silence by opening up to me about his life, in hopes that I would eventually do the same. I knew he wanted answers to this great mystery of his life, but I was not ready to speak of my ordeal. I kept my head down and took in the night air. I remember the Judge had a special pair of shoes that wrapped around his feet and cushioned the step so there was less tension in his aging bones. He noticed my admiring gaze and arranged a pair for me. When I first used them, I was able to walk as if I was twenty years old again. It was an amazing experience initially, but then each time I wore them and felt my spryness return, I began to feel immense guilt and shame for enjoying myself.

My guardian lived alone in a building designated for his high ranking position in the courts. While I never entered his living quarters, I can only imagine that they were quite luxurious. The Judge had a fine style in his tailored linen clothing, and always appeared well groomed. He was a smaller man, roundish with half moon glasses and a tuft of silvery grey hair traveling from ear to ear. Over time, I came to understand that he was the only child of a well known Atlantean politician and his emotionally distant wife. His father saw to it that the Judge's education was geared towards this profession and no expense was spared in achieving this goal. Private tutors were some of the only people he saw during a lonely childhood marked by periods of isolation due to the virus of Atlantis. I came to understand that as the Judge grew into adulthood, he was told he must marry, and so he married a woman he thought he could love. I believe she died in the early stages of her pregnancy with their first child. I felt he filled this void of companionship with the time he spent serving the high courts of Atlantis.

During the day, the Judge worked constantly trying to figure out what to do with the Animal People of Atlantis. This case was an ongoing saga the Judge had been involved in for many generations. The Judge talked of the day we met and explained that it was on this day that the Atlanteans were celebrating a victory of science. A vaccine had been developed for the virus, and for the first time in years, the upper echelon of society were gathered together without fear of transmission. It was a brief golden period for Osiris as the vaccine was administered to the people of Atlantis and life went back to normal. Inoculations were widespread, starting with the wealthiest tier of citizens. Initially, the vaccine had few side effects and was hailed a success. Eventually, the virus disappeared from society. It took quite a few years before the children who were administered the vaccine were old enough to have children of their own.

The Judge described to me the plague of negative results that started appearing within their society, and how children were born with things that they should not have been born with. Amongst the first grouping of children born to these vaccine recipients, there were children who appeared to have reptilian skin, other groupings could breathe underwater, while others had spry feline physical attributes. Some even had strangely patterned markings on their skin that caused burns on those who held them.

I learned that the Atlanteans were forced to stop administering the vaccine, and as a result the virus found its way back into the population. Their scientists rapidly searched for a way to restructure their vaccine without the occurrence of the human-animal hybrids. It took many years before they found a sequencing that they believed would work, and cautiously administered it to the people of Atlantis. They believed they had finally won their battle against the ravages of the virus. Though as time passed, the Judge said they were forced to confront their failure with the second vaccine when more children with animal features were born a generation later to those vaccine recipients. This time the animal features were stronger, with heightened powers noticed amongst the infants rounded up. Osiris saw this as a mark on his great society and ordered the babies removed from their mothers at birth if they showed animal characteristics. Many were taken away from their parents and killed. Some of the children in the rural parts of Atlantis were killed by their families because it became such a stigmatic thing to have associated with your family name.

Some of the Animal People who were not murdered in their infancy were sent to facilities like the one I was kept in to be studied. They were subject to intrusive laboratory testing and inhumanly treated as if they had been responsible for their bodies at birth. The experimenting yielded no clues to the scientists in finding a cure for the virus, nor the vaccine. As the Animal Children grew and learned how they were not welcomed in their society, they began to react to their environment, and lash out. These violent acts only further ostracized them from the elitist Atlantean society.

There developed a deep dischord in their land over this as generations passed and a surge of Animal Children were born into their society. The mutation was hidden deep within recipients of the earlier vaccines, and sporadically these hybrids were born to their descendants. I understood that a usable vaccine was eventually developed, and with it the virus mostly subsided, but still remaining was the problem of the Animal People.

The Judge was not alone in his quest to bring justice to the Animal People. He spent his time during the day with two other male judges. Together, they formed a triumvirate that oversaw the highest courts of Atlantis. The trio had worked together for many years and treated each other as family. The three Judges consulted each other on how the Animal People should be treated and what their fates should be. In the past, the three were not sure of how to handle the hybrids, and debated if they should allow them to continue being Atlanteans, or if they should all together be removed from society's view. The Judges ultimately decided the hybrids that were able to hide their physical differences were to be kept within Atlantis. The Animal People that had obvious physical and mental alterations were sent away to a colony housed on a remote island off the coast of Atlantis.

For years Animal People were sent to the secluded island under the pretense that it housed a facility with resources to house and care for them. And so they were separated from their families and sent away. I was told by an impassioned Judge that children were torn from the arms of the loving parents who had hidden them away to protect them. Their families protested and begged for justice. It wore heavy on the Judges, and the three deciders hit a point where they began to question if the separation was something that needed to continue. In order to make a well informed decision, the Judge told me he set out on a journey with the other judges to the island of the Animal People, to see for themselves the entire situation at hand.

The Judge and I walked by the water one night as he described his experience on the small wooden ferry that carried the trio to the island on a cold winter's day. Suspicions grew when they first approached the ferry to travel to the island, and the captain tried to stop their passage. The Judges insisted on passage and boarded the boat as the government officials were alerted to their presence on the ferry. After a nauseating trip over choppy water, the judges arrived to find a desolate island void of life. The only structure on the island was the shell of an old grey stone building with no roof that stretched for nearly half a mile. Inside, it was empty, except for a chalky gray dust that was piled everywhere.

The Judge recounted that it was a very windy day, and dust was swirling all around as they searched for any sign of life on the island. The grey dust infiltrated around them, blinding their eyes and filling their mouths and noses as they coughed violently. It was in the midst of their inability to breathe, that the Judge realized that the dust they were being attacked by was all that was left of the Animal People they had banished to the island.

The judges now understood it was a death sentence to go to the island, and they demanded Osiris shut the program down immediately. Hundreds of thousands of lives had already been sent there and they refused to allow one more to cross its threshold. The Judge believed that with these demands, the government took careful attention to destroy any evidence, and burned the island down to its coral rock base. With this, the Island of the Animal People was shut down for good, but the ordeal was far from over for the judges. As a mode to discredit them, Osiris had their grey judges' robes stricken, and all three were silenced with threats of violence, and subsequently forced into retirement.

The tyrannical treatment of the Animal People continued until fate saw to it that the only grandchild of Osiris was born with prominent Cat People features. The Judge often remarked on the hypocrisy he witnessed when Osiris held firm to his policies towards the Animal People in his public life, yet privately sought to protect the child from the fate of her kind. Because of her secret confinement, Osiris was able to see that his grandchild had a strange intelligence when it came to things such as crystals and conductivity. Using all kinds of crystals, the Animal People could manipulate a previously unknown energy source and channel it through their bodies. As he watched the electrical magic she could perform, he realized that they had been killing off the answer to their problem.

The Atlantean scientists dedicated themselves to studying this new energy and their curiosity directed the hybridization program in a new direction. This time, instead of killing the Animal People quickly with the light, they tested their conductivity powers with many prolonged torturous equipment. Those of the Animal People who did not have the desired features to conduct the new electricity were sent back into Atlantean society, but were never treated as humans or considered equal by any means. They were forced to live beyond the outermost ring of Atlantis and keep to themselves so they might hide their truth.

With the death of Osiris and the fall of his

bitter dictatorship, the new government had re-instated the Judge to his high ranking position. Arion, the new leader of Atlantis, claimed to want change and allowed the Judges to proceed with the dealings of the Animal People, and the new challenges faced integrating them.

In order to allow for greater flexibility in the Judges schedule, a small device was placed in my leg and tracked my whereabouts. With this new invasion of privacy came greater freedom. I was given permission to travel during the daylight within the city center. I began to journey with the Judge every so often to his offices at the Halls of Justice. As we walked to the towering building, I could see things unnoticeable in the darkness of our nightime walks. There was a floating trolley that traveled the inner rings of Atlantis and com-muted many citizens to their various purposes.

I was shocked and delighted to see many of the rare plants from our palace gardens in Amun growing freely in the many parks that beautified the capitol. Pyramid structures dotted the land-scape beyond the inner ring. The Judge said they were used to store the energy that was harnessed from the sun and moon that powered Atlantis. No matter the time of day that we walked together, the Judge always passed the same spot, an em-bankment on the side of a bridge that once housed the restaurant where we first met. Over the years it had transformed from a restaurant for the elite into a small park that grew beautifully colored flowers in long concrete planters along the sea-wall.

My visits to the Halls of Justice were always difficult to swallow. I could not help but be impressed with their craftsmanship and design. Outside, the building's facade was made of white marble that had carved into it the ancient history of Atlantis. Inside the building, there was a long white corridor amongst marble pillars of pure white that led to the offices of the three judges. There were numerous documents on the walls of the corridor that looked very old and were protected behind thick glass frames. On the wall outside the office of the Judge was a large glass box that held an ancient document of the written laws of Atlantis from earlier times. Above this hung banners of white and burgundy with "Sacrifice Oneself for the Betterment of Society" in ancient Atlantean written on them.

The Judge's office was filled with glossy dark wood furniture and bookcases that lined the walls. Ivory and deep reds decorated the windows, while books piled everywhere gave off a hoarder's quality to his work. Ornate crystal light fixtures hung down from the ceiling in all their prismatic wonder. The Judge remarked that the chandeliers were made from a very special crystal that was believed to bring clarity to those around it.

There was a young woman in the office that worked with him and the other judges. Her name was Devika, she was brought in to learn the laws of Atlantis. Devika was the granddaughter of one of the other Judges in the trio and was expected to continue in the family tradition. I remember the first time I saw her as she traveled up and down the long marble corridor that led to the Judges offices. Hurriedly, she walked past and glanced as if she knew me, but quickly turned and avoided my gaze when I made eye contact. Her white blonde hair gave her the look of an Atlantean but below her skeptical eyebrows were dark eyes so intense that they almost appeared black. Her Atlantean roots were deep, and I could feel her sense of entitlement and superiority pulsing through her superficially calm demeanor. She was no more than fifteen years when I first saw her, still unknowing of her own beliefs but proud to regurgitate the beliefs of others she had been told to respect.

There was a saying in Amun that I heard often in my youth: "the child who is not embraced by the village will burn it down to feel its warmth." This saying always reminded me of Devika and her journey into my life. It was an evening not long after our first meeting that her life was to change forever and our paths would be forged together. As she travelled to her grandfather's home to attend a family gathering, Devika was held up by a strange accident that blocked her way and arrived at the dinner later than planned. All her relations had sat down at the highly polished wooden table and had begun eating their dinner.

Devika found her place and was about to join their eating when she heard a strange coughing sound come from the other end of the table. All eyes were on her grandfather, who was turning many shades of red and gasping for breath. Devika believed he was choking and rushed to assist him. Instead of dislodging a piece of food, her grandfather spewed volumes of blood from his mouth and then collapsed in his dinner plate. As Devika looked up to find assistance from amongst her family, to her horror, she saw the same fate repeated on each of them. Within moments, they were all gone, and she was suddenly alone in the world.

The new Atlantean government did their investigation and claimed the poisoning was a rogue agent seeking revenge on her high-ranking grandfather and his family. I could tell Devika knew better than to believe that explanation. She had worked closely with her grandfather and knew of the duplicity that lined the inner workings of the government. She was wise to see that the new Atlantean leader, Arion, was not the progressive statesman he presented to the public. He was charming and smart, but his confidence was a well-orchestrated event. Arion was the face of the new Atlantis, he claimed to be the light that would guide the way to a golden age. Devika had grown up in the same circles as Arion and knew he was nothing more than a puppet for their dead dictator.

The Judge knew Devika was not safe on her own, and so he was granted custody of the young woman. Devika stayed with him in his high-rise apartment and refused to go outside her room or speak with anyone but the Judge. Devika understood what happened to her family, and knew she was one small accident away from joining them.

The Judge kindly encouraged Devika to join us on our nightly walks, and eventually she broke free from her self-imposed prison and began to join us. The first time we walked together I could feel the hatred for the Atlanteans in her. It was the same hatred I felt, and I could not help but relate to her. We walked in silence one night near the spot where the restaurant on the side of the bridge once stood. Something caught the corner of my eye, it was like a subtle spark of yellow light emanating from just behind me. As I turned to see the source of this spark, I carelessly twisted my ankle on the cobblestone street. Being near, Devika instinctively reached for my hand to prevent my fall. As her pale fingers touched mine, a powerful electrical shock was felt between the two of us. My hair stood up on end as I am sure hers did as well.

The doctor insisted I must remain off my feet, and so the Judge asked Devika to assist me for a few days while I recovered. The next morning, she quietly entered my modest quarters and began to arrange my morning meal. When Devika entered my room and placed the tray in front of me I was overwhelmed to see that in the middle of the bowl of food was a small purple flower. As a young child, my grandmother would often pick the same flowers from the special trees in her private gardens of the palace.

The Queen would send them to the kitchens to have placed on my food as a special treat. The flowers were edible and tasted like spun sugar. As I ate that purple flower, I began to cry. Uncomfortable by my show of emotion, Devika left abruptly, but true to her word, she returned midday to help prepare my next meal. Once again she approached me with a tray, but stumbled and spilled some of the food onto the floor in front of me. As we both reached to clean the mess, once again our hands touched. With a flourishing spark, the strange yellow energy presented itself once more. I could tell it stung Devika as much as it did me when she coiled away like a jungle cat that needed to lick its wounds.

We both stared at each other until I motioned for her to sit in the chair across from me. She left the mess on the floor and joined me at the table. It was a natural meditation as we sat there with the center of our foreheads directly facing each other. It was necessary to have quite a few feet between us so that the energy would not backfire and harm either one of us. We did not converse with each other, we did not need to. I closed my eyes and relaxed so the transmission of power could begin. It was not a hard process for me to let go of this energy, but a hard process for her to accept it. Devika seemed to have understood that this was going to happen, it felt as if she was born programmed to take on this power. I can see that she has spent her young life filled with a feeling that was the opposite of the feeling that I had growing up. While I knew that it was always going to end with me, she had always known that it would begin with her.

I was surprised when she allowed me to view her life and shared with me her truth. Devika was an Animal Person, and though she showed very subtle outward feline signs, she was a recipient of immense inner abilities. Devika knew why her family was killed. It was meant to remove the obstacles her high ranking grandfather had placed in the way to stop her from being taken by the government. She believed they were coming for her, coming for her powers. I knew what tortures awaited her in their laboratories, I knew I had to get her out of Atlantis.

To begin the process I first transmitted the memory of Evi and Commander Attoms to Devika. She received it well and I continued to work with her on the specific meditations and traveling through to communicate with the other side. It was harder for her to do the meditations, she was confused by what she saw on the other side and could not see it as clearly or communicate with them as deeply. There was much to accomplish and I could feel my end approaching. Devika had received some of my powers, but I suddenly worried this power might cause her trouble as it has caused much for me. I decided she must receive the memory of the Wave. She must know what her people are responsible for before I unload the rest of my powers.

I could not let her take on something so immense, and not know what people would destroy to possess it. I felt the pain of the wave leave my mind as the young girl saw in clear eyes what her society was. The veil had been lifted and the lie she had been fed her entire life was now exposed. An overwhelming disgust took over her body and she refused to participate in my transfer any further. She said it was too much, too great a responsibility. I could feel her mind was shut tight and fighting the energy I was trying to give her. This was not something that could be forced onto another, so I immediately halted my transmission. I was disappointed and felt the sting of failure for not having fulfilled my mission in transferring all of my powers.

As I walked with Devika and the Judge around the innermost ring of Atlantis later that night, transport spheres suddenly descended and Devka was taken from us. The armed guards of Atlantis knocked the Judge and I to the ground and held us against the cobblestones with their feet on our backs. We watched powerlessly as a black woven bag was thrown over Devika's head and her arms and legs forcefully tied behind her. The girl was hurriedly tossed into a transport sphere as the Judge and I were mercilessly knocked unconscious with batons by the guards.

In my feeble comatose state I dreamt of my mother, Queen Sunisa. She stood proudly before me with her crown and staff but said nothing, her face was frozen in a stony glare. In her eyes I could see something glimmer, but could not see the image with clarity. As I looked closer I could see the outline of a massive explosion within the black centers of her knowing eyes. When I awoke, I was disoriented and it took a moment for me to realize I was in my small quarters. The Judge remained unconscious on the floor in front of my window. I knew what would have to be done, and as soon as the Judge was able to regain his standing, I had him send word through the spying box that I had information for their leader Arion regarding his Red Crystal. The protege of Osiris must have been intrigued because it was not long before the Judge and I were both thrown into transport spheres and left Poseida for the last time.

On a small island off the south west coast of Atlantis there stood a massive facility that was built to house the new energy of Atlantis. When I arrived at the facility, I could feel what the place truly was before I even entered the building. My torture and experiments had only been a precursor to their scientific breakthroughs, and this facility was the ultimate cumulation of what they had uncovered of the Red Crystal since my capture. Inside the thick walls of the windowless facility housed a breeding program for creating specialized Animal People to conduct the new energy of Atlantis.

Neglected Animal Children filled the endless facility. They all had dark circles under their eyes, badly stuttered, and twitched in their shrivelled little bodies. The creation of energy in this facility was channeled through them and as a result, sucked the life out of them.

When I arrived, wealthy people of Atlantis were visiting the facility to have rejuvenating treatments done with this energy source. A single treatment would create a short lived cure for all their ailments and revive their bodies with pure health. It had the potential to prolong their life indefinitely, creating an endless need for the enslaved Animal Children. Those Atlanteans I saw in the facility who received the treatments were very aware of how this energy was processed and undoubtedly would continue to cycle back with reckless abandonment. It was shameful to see all of this dysfunction to benefit just a few. They kept Devika in this facility for days, torturing her with all kinds of invasive exams and electrical shocks. This was just the beginning of their plans for her. Should they be successful, she would give birth to numerous children that would be ripped from her womb and strapped into the energy system.

The new ruler of Atlantis traveled to the

island to meet with me. I could easily see why Osiris had hand-picked the young man to rule. While on the outside Arion looked and acted the face of modernity and freedom the Atlanteans craved, he was inside nothing more than the same disingenuous rot that Osiris had embodied. As he stood across from me I could feel that Osiris had been grooming Arion for this his entire life. As I looked further into his soul, I saw this was an unfulfilled life for him, Arion had spent his life taking orders from a tyrant and performing his appalling tasks with the promise that one day he would do things right when he had the chance. As time passed he learned of the power of the Red Crystal, and instead fell deep into its abyss.

I told him I had one condition in handing over the information, that Devika would be allowed to leave the facility. Arion agreed, but I could clearly see his promises were all lies and knew his guards would instead hunt Devika down as soon as they had extracted the information from me. As I agreed to Arion's terms, the Judge was roughly dragged away and detained in a small prison built next to the facility. The prison had been constructed for those who travelled to the island and did not agree with what they saw. It was Arion's intention to leave the meddlesome Judge there for however long his life might be. As long as he was within the walls of the island prison, the Judge was one less person to blow the whistle on this covert energy project. When the

Judge was violently pulled away from me, I knew it was the last time I would ever see him. We locked eyes despite the turmoil around us and I inwardly felt his message: "It is time to go home."

The Judge looked pained but did not fight the guards as they dragged him from the facility. I did nothing to save him. We both understood when we arrived that we would not be leaving the island. Before I began, I demanded proof of life for Devika from Arion. She was brought to me and roughly dumped at my feet by two guards. I hardly recognized the girl brought before me and my heart ached at the sight of her shaved head and bruises. I said nothing to her but instead gave her the woolen jacket I wore.

As I stood silently across from her I transmitted the memory of the words Oona said to me during my last meditation: "She must go to the north of the island and climb the mountain. Go as far as possible, until she sees only snow." Devika received the memory, and then with a sudden rush of adrenaline, she turned and ran from the building. The guards swiftly closed and locked the heavy metal doors behind her. Arion looked to me to begin my explanation of the Red Crystals energy. I told the leader and his team of scientists that the power was best explained and utilized at sunrise, and we would have to wait until then to proceed. He begrudgingly agreed and threw a small tantrum that reminded me of Osiris in his youth. That night, for the last time, I was locked into a cell. Sometime before sunrise, the guards woke me from my sleep. For a brief moment, I felt that it was the day of the wave, that the water was missing again and my guards were waking me, but it only took a moment to brush this feeling aside. Today was going to be a very different day.

I was led by a vibrantly beaming Arion down many echoing corridors into the depths of the vile powerhouse. Hidden away within the heart of the facility was the Red Crystal my mother had gifted as a gesture of good will to Osiris. It felt like it had been another life when that crystal had been gifted to my mother's assassin. The gem now served as the conduit for their energy project with the Animal People, and without it, all efforts to harness the rejuvenating energy were futile. I could feel the Red Crystal's power growing as we grew in proximity.

The Atlanteans kept the crystal on a platform made of metal, and enclosed it in a clear dome that protected those who could not channel the energy. I left behind Arion and approached the crystal as one would an old friend. I lifted the dome and I could feel the crystal's heat as I held my hands above it. My fingers lovingly felt the many familiar facets of the crystal as I picked it up and held it to my chest. I closed my eyes for the last time and began to take in the energy of the Red Crystal. I could see what they had unknowingly created with the power of the Red Crystal as they conducted it through the Animal

People. Though the scientists could not understand what it was, I gladly recognized the passageway to the otherside my grandmother had guided me through in my youth. As I meditated and journeyed to the otherside, I saw again the leaking door from the terrifying meditations of my youth. This time, I was not afraid. I approached the nearly bursting door without fear and pulled it wide open.

Instead of water, an immense light shot out from the door. For just a moment, I felt it cut right into me. It was painful, but it was something I wanted to feel. I suddenly experienced this immense freedom and unexpected happiness. I could feel my blood pulsing with the energy of the Red Crystal, and then suddenly, there was a sensation that I was encapsulated by a concrete womb. And then I felt it release from my body, drain out like a wave washing from my head to toes. The Red Crystal misfired and caused the most beautiful explosion. Over the course of a day, it blew the entire civilization and most of its inhabitants into bits and pieces.

They let me watch it from above as explosions occurred all over Atlantis. The island cracked like a dropped egg and swallowed up thousands without warning. From the tops of the many pyramids that supplied energy to the people of Atlantis surged columns of boiling steam that scalded their surroundings. Massive explosions continued throughout the island until

sunset submerged the few who survived the cataclysm into darkness. Before the light of day would
appear again, Atlantis was gone, erased from history. As I hovered in my spirit form and watched, I
felt complete. I knew it was time to go home.

In all of my lives, I had never been so happy
to die.

EPILOGUE

I always knew it would end with me, but with each end a new beginning is born. Over time, I have learned that on that fateful day, Devika ran from the towering walls that encircled the facility and did not look back. Ahead to the North she could see the gray mountain she was to climb and followed my message. She had no shoes on her feet and only a thin medical gown and my jacket to protect her. The cold moist wind blew at her back and pushed her, even lifted her at times towards the mountain. Devika ran further and harder, stumbling on the sharp incline but continuing with the ferocity of a feral animal.

Devika knew she had little time before the guards would be sent to track and hunt her down. As the sun began to set, the air chilled and freezing cold rain stung her face. Still, she persisted and fought the mountain. Before the first rays of dawn appeared, the rain transformed into snow and began to swirl around her in a blinding whirlwind. Devika's instinct to keep moving propelled her forward even though she was nearly frozen. She put one foot in front of the other and kept moving until snow blinded her sight, and the hard rocky ground disappeared beneath her.

Without warning, Devika slid down into a mountainous void at breakneck speed. She tried to hold onto anything to stop her from slipping further down the hole, yet found nothing but snow and smooth rock. Headfirst she plummeted downward into the mountain cave. Sure of her impending death, Devika closed her eyes and braced for impact. With her eyes closed to the world she did not see the stone circle that lay at the bottom of this cave. Built by some of the earliest colonizers from the home planet, the stone circle Chasm activated as Devika free fell through it. A vortex opened and her body was transported before she hit the ground beneath the stone circle.

With her eyes still clenched shut, she landed with a thud on the muddy grass in the center of a distinctly different stone circle. When she was sure she was not dead, Devika's black eyes opened to see a gathering of people around her, curiously watching her with amazement. Next to where she had fallen was a small formation of Red Crystals arranged on a rock altar that the stone circle was built around. Devika appeared as a god to the people of this land, falling from the sky into their lives with her immense powers. She was welcomed and loved by these people and used the Red Crystals to guide and protect them. On a mysterious island that was surrounded by a calm green sea, Devika's descendents ruled for generations as the world beyond healed from the loss of Amun and Atlantis.

Thousands of years have passed since these cataclysms. Many times I have been reborn and born again, only to remember and forget my sordid past with each incarnation. Over and over again I have tried and failed to bring back to our collective consciousness the lost history of our true origin. I have a new body now, and often in her dreams I float above the ocean and look at how the shape of everything has changed so much over the years. When I look down, I can see where Atlantis once was is now a giant blue crater under the ocean that has filled with the shifting debris of time. In the warm waters near the facility where I died, strange things happen to those who travel through. Many go missing into the watery abyss, never to be seen again. I believe the Red Crystal is still down there, waiting to be used once more.

I sometimes go to where the palace of Amun once was. When I visit there, it feels like I am home. There is a small stilted house built on top of the blue-green water. The pristine water runs underneath the house and cradles the bamboo poles holding the structure up in the shallow water. It feels very comforting to be there, very peaceful. I want to put my feet in the water and once again be on the narrow beach outside my palace room, but I know that is not possible. Crumbling beneath the water that covers my homeland are the remnants of the faces of the leaders of Amun carved into megalithic boulders. The profiles of my ancestors are cracked and covered in many layers of mud in a place where no one knows what lies beneath the sandy blue waters they swim above.

It is hard to visit the cave of the Red Crystals now and see the crystals sitting alone on their altar. When I hold them they transmit the memories of my people, and they send a deep echoing sadness outwards. The direct memories of millions are trapped in these crystals because they died so suddenly and still do not know they are gone. I have tried my best to free these souls, but I have learned over time that one is ever truly free until they have freed themselves. As I look over this lifetime, I can now see it for what it was, an organized, predestined, and necessary experience. I feel my soul is now relieved of this heavy burden. And with this story's end, I have become unchained from my earthly shackles, and may be lifted to take my rightful place as a child of the Universe.

❋ ❋ ❋

WANT TO KNOW MORE?

For additional information regarding the 2018-2020 QHHT sessions that *Child Of The Universe* originated from, please read the companion novel:

"A Hypnotist's Journey To Atlantis,"
by Sarah Breskman Cosme